CW00863987

The Stones of Earth and Air

THE STONES OF
EARTH AND AIR

Elemental Worlds Book I

V. M. Sang

Copyright (C) 2017 V.M. Sang
Layout design and Copyright (C) 2017 Creativia
Published 2017 by Creativia (www.creativia.org)
Cover art by Cover Mint
This book is a work of fiction. Names, characters, places, and incidents are the product of the author's imagination or are used fictitiously. Any resemblance to actual events, locales, or persons, living or dead, is purely coincidental.
All rights reserved. No part of this book may be reproduced or transmitted in any form or by any means, electronic or mechanical, including photocopying, recording, or by any information storage and retrieval system, without the author's permission.

Other books by VM Sang

Fiction

The Wolves of Vimar Series

Book 1 - The Wolf Pack

Book 2 - The Never-Dying Man

Non-fiction

Viv's Family Recipes

A collection of recipes gathered by friends and family over 100 years. There are some interesting insights into the people who collected them as well as the recipes themselves.

Terra

Chapter 1

The large, grey wolfhound growled as the Crown Prince of Ponderia entered the room. The prince scowled at the dog.

'Shut that animal up, Pettic. He knows me well enough. Why is he growling at me?'

'I really don't know, Torren,' replied the blonde young man sitting near the window.

He put a restraining hand on the dog's neck and said, 'Be quiet, Cledo. You know the prince and you like him.' He turned to the prince. 'I can't understand it. He usually greets you as eagerly as he greets me. I don't know what's got into him.'

'Well, if you can't get him to stop being so savage, he'll have to be put down. And you shouldn't call me by my name now I'm eighteen. I'm a prince and you're a commoner after all. I've been invested as Crown Prince and will be taking on some of my father's duties from now on.'

With that, the prince threw himself into a chair by the fireplace opposite where the children's nurse sat, telling a story to the youngest of the family, six-year-old Prince Allry.

'You shouldn't talk to Pettic like that.' This was sixteen-year-old Princess Lucenra. 'He's been a good friend to you for the last five years. Remember you chose him yourself from among the boys brought to you on your thirteenth birthday. It was you who insisted that the fact he's a commoner didn't matter when father suggested one of the sons of the nobility would be a better companion for a prince. The pair of you've been inseparable ever since. You even gave him the dog for his sixteenth birthday.'

The two young men were exactly the same age. On Prince Torren's thirteenth birthday the king allowed him to choose a companion from amongst many boys who shared his birthday. The boys had come to Glitton, the capital city of Ponderia, from all around the country in response to a proclamation. Prince Torren and Pettic had immediately formed a bond and the young prince would not be swayed from his choice.

Everyone agreed in the intervening years that the choice had been a good one, each boy complementing a trait in the other. Prince Torren had been self-confident and he had helped Pettic to gain his own confidence. Pettic, in his turn had helped the prince to realise that ordinary people were not any different from royalty and the prince had spent many happy hours at Pettic's parent's farm, helping with the various chores. Now it seemed the bond was breaking down.

Lucenra continued scolding the prince, and the two younger princes and the other princess stopped what they were doing to listen.

'Luce is right, Torren,' called fourteen year old princess Icerra. 'He's been your best friend for ages. You shouldn't speak to him like that, nor insist he stops calling you by your name.'

The two younger boys, Prince Phillus and Prince Kitu both nodded their agreement. So did the nurse, but she refrained from saying anything aloud, having been on the receiving end of a tongue-lashing from Prince Torren the previous day. This culminated in a threatened firing from the prince—a fact that had shocked the old woman because she had brought up all six of the royal children from birth, and they all loved her greatly.

On seeing all his siblings seemed to be against him, Prince Torren stormed out of the nursery and off to his own apartments. The king gave Torren and Pettic their own rooms the previous year. Apartments opposite each other in the palace.

As soon as Torren left, Cledo stopped growling and settled down again. Pettic rose to leave, but Princess Lucenra stopped him.

'Please stay, Pettic. I'd like to talk to you.'

Pettic sat down again. Cledo wagged his tail as the princess came and sat next to him. She bent down and stroked the dog's head.

'There's something very wrong with Torren,' she began. 'I'd almost believe it isn't him he's so different. He was never so arrogant and conscious of being a prince, and he'd never have told you to stop calling him by his given name in the past. It's come on him so quickly that I wonder if somehow he could be under a spell.'

'We could go to see Blundo,' suggested Pettic, naming the court magician. 'He might know if such a thing is possible.'

Princess Lucenra jumped up immediately. 'A good idea,' she said. 'Let's go now.'

She immediately started heading for the door and Pettic had to hurry to catch up with her.

They made their way along the maze of corridors in the palace to where a spiral staircase rose up to a tower room. There they knocked and a voice told them to enter.

The room was full of clutter, at least to the uninitiated, but Pettic supposed that to a magician it all made sense. There were bottles and boxes all around and books on every surface. The dried remains of a variety of animals hung from the ceiling and various contraptions stood on tables and chairs.

The window looked over the town, and stood open in spite of the winter chill in the air. The remains of smoke hung in the room, which accounted for the open window. A slightly sweet-ish odour that Pettic could not place drifted to his nostrils

Leaning over a bench where the smoke appeared to have come from, was a youngish man. He appeared to be in his mid thirties with brown hair that he wore longer than usual. Whether this was from preference or from forgetting to get it cut no one knew.

He wore a brown robe tied in the middle with a piece of string in lieu of a belt. As the pair approached him, he turned and smiled, making his whole face light up.

'Well, if it isn't Princess Lucenra and Earl Pettic! Welcome, Your Highness, and My Lord. To what do I owe the pleasure of this visit?'

Lucenra answered him. 'We have come to ask you if something is possible using magic.'

'What is it you want to know?'

Pettic cut in. 'We wondered if it's possible to change someone's personality using a spell,' he said.

'Well, now,' the magician mused, frowning. 'That all depends on exactly what you want to accomplish. A complete change isn't really possible, but it is possible to bring out latent personality traits.'

He paused and scratched his head. 'It's also possible to get someone to do something for you, as a favour—to make them like you enough to do almost anything for you, but these are all short-lasting spells. What is it you want to do?'

'It's not us,' said Pettic, 'but Prince Torren seems to be behaving very much out of character. I've been his best friend for the past five years now and Lucenra's his sister. We're both seeing a side of him he's never exhibited before. He's arrogant, thoughtless and even on occasion cruel. He threatened Nurse with being fired yesterday, and we all know how much he's always loved her.'

'Hmm. That doesn't sound like Prince Torren. Leave it with me and I'll look in my library and see what I can find. Come back tomorrow afternoon and I'll tell you if I've discovered anything.'

The next afternoon Lucenra and Pettic climbed the stairs to the magician's room once more. They knocked on the door and Blundo bade them enter. They found him poring over a book. This time the window was closed and a fire burned in the fireplace making it cosy and warm. Blundo stood up as they entered and sketched a bow towards the princess.

'I think I may have found out something that would work, but as to the why, I've no idea,' he said. 'It's possible to change a person's appearance.'

He walked over and picked up a large book from one of the bookshelves before continuing.

'Now, if someone wanted to replace one person with another, they could do this, but it would mean enchanting a gem for the person to wear. Even so, the spell is not permanent.' He frowned. 'This would mean the gem would have to be re-enchanted every so often. How long the spell lasts would depend on the strength of the magician concerned. Have you noticed the prince going away on his own at all?'

'Not really,' replied Lucenra, walking around the room and looking at things. She picked up a gem lying on a table. It tingled in her hand and so surprised her she almost dropped it.

Blundo looked at her.

'Did you feel something? he asked.

'It seemed to tingle,' she replied, frowning, 'but that's not possible.'

'Yes it is if you have an affinity for the gems,' replied Blundo, taking it from her. 'A pity you're a royal princess. That tingle implies you could become a magician.'

Then Pettic interrupted. 'I was just thinking. There was one occasion when Torren took his horse and went off. I asked him to wait so I could saddle mine and accompany him but he told me he wanted to have a ride by himself. I thought this was odd because he always wants me to accompany him on his rides.'

Both Lucenra and Blundo looked at him.

'When was this?' asked Blundo.

He shrugged. 'About three or four weeks ago, I think.'

'Hmm!' Blundo stroked his chin, which he wore clean-shaven, unlike many magicians. 'Watch him very carefully and if he goes off again on his own, try to follow him. See where he goes and whom he meets and look for any signs that magic is being used. Someone doing something with a gem, that sort of thing, then come back to me and we'll talk again.'

It was almost a week later that Torren went off again. He announced he was going for a walk and he wanted to go alone.

Fourteen-year-old Icerra tossed her black hair and grinned. 'Who is she, Torren?' she giggled. 'That's the third time you've gone off on your own. But she can't be so wonderful, because you only see her every few weeks!'

Torren rounded on his sister. 'It's not a girl!' he stormed. 'If I want to go for a walk on my own, I can go for a walk on my own. It's none of your business.' He turned to the others, 'And yes, before you say anything I know it's snowing out there. I LIKE walking in the snow.'

With that, he swept out of the nursery where, out of habit, he and Lucenra still gathered along with Pettic, even though all had their own rooms now.

'Time to follow, Pettic,' whispered Lucenra, and Pettic stood up and casually left the room, picking up a warm cloak as he passed the cloak stand.

Torren left the building and crossed the palace gardens to a small gate in the wall. Few people used this gate and most had forgotten its existence. The children used it when they wanted to escape the wrath of someone in the palace. He passed through and into the streets of the city. He did not see the shadow slip through after him.

The narrow path leading away from the little gate led to some narrow back streets. They were rarely inhabited and so, as the children had found out in earlier years, they could easily pass unnoticed through the city streets. Fortunately for Pettic, the snow made it easy for him to track Torren, and the dark, narrow alleyways meant he could keep hidden.

Torren came to a gate out of the city. He had a cloak wrapped tightly round him and the guards did not recognise him as he passed through. The guards did recognise Pettic, though They knew him well and waved at him. They assumed he was going into the city to buy something, or some other errand.

Pettic followed Torren along the road for a little way,being sure to keep hidden, until the prince turned off the road into the forest. After a few minutes walking, he turned up what looked like a deer track. Pettic followed keeping his distance. It was easy to remain hidden amongst the trees, and anyway, Torren never looked back.

After half an hour's walking they came to a clearing where a heavily cloaked man waited. Torren approached the man and mumbled something Pettic could not catch, and he crept as near as he dared, hiding behind the bushes that grew under the trees.

The man said, 'Well Dilrong, is it going as planned?'

'Yes. No one suspects anything.'

'Time to replenish the spell then. Give me the ring.'

When Torren, who it seemed was called Dilrong, handed over his ring, the prince seemed to disappear and a different young man stood in his place. Although he was about the same height as the Prince, there all resemblence ended. This person had un-ruly, mousy hair and a rather sly look to his face. It was a look that Pettic had noticed on the prince in the last few months. He had a longer nose than Torren and a rather pinched mouth.

The strange man took a contraption from beneath his cloak which he put on the ground. He suspended the ring on a chain so it hung down inside. Then the muffled up man started mumbling and a light appeared in the contraption.

'Can't you make the spell last longer?' Dilrong asked.

The magician ignored the young man for a few minutes, took the ring from the contraption and handed it back. As soon as he put the ring back on, Prince Torren once more stood in the clearing.

'I know having to come out here every few weeks is a nuisance, but being Crown Prince, and ultimately King, will be well worth it, I think you'll agree.'

So it isn't Torren. We were right. But why has this magician (for he must be a magician) done this? And who is he? Pettic wondered.

Pettic hurried back to the palace to tell Lucenra all he had found out. He found her in her rooms when he got there, getting ready for the evening meal with her parents and he had no chance of speaking to her.

He entered his own rooms and threw his wet cloak down on the floor. He was not customarily untidy, nor inconsiderate of the servants, but he felt frustrated. He needed to talk to someone about what he had seen. He realised it was getting late so he rang for his valet and asked him to prepare a bath and lay out his clothes for the evening.

He went to meet the royal children in the nursery as usual before going to dinner. As it happened he was a little early and met Lucenra and Icerra just outside the door. The boys had not yet arrived. As he went to open the door, someone opened it from the other side and there stood Blundo.

For a few minutes they all stood looking at each other, then Lucenra said, 'What are you doing in the nursery?'

Blundo looked at the princess then cast his eyes down as he remembered to bow.

'Err…you remember the enchanted crystals my predecessor gave you as protection?' he said quickly. 'Well, I've only just found out about them so I came straight away to check they were still there and the enchantment's still holding.'

'And is it?' replied the princess.

'Yes, your Highness. You'll be pleased to know it's holding very well.'

He bowed again and left. By then, the others had arrived and they all went down to the small hall for dinner.

After dinner there was to be a concert in the Great Hall by a well-known quartet and the king and queen expected Pettic to be there with Torren. He was looking forward to it as he enjoyed music. He knew Torren would not have been, though, as he was not very musical. Would this other 'Torren' enjoy the concert, he wondered?

Chapter 2

Dinner was pleasant. Torren, or Dilrong, he supposed he should think of him now, sat at the other end of the table from Pettic, close to the daughter of the Duke of Kroldor. She was a pretty girl and Torren was paying her close attention and turning on the charm. He hardly noticed Pettic, gracing him with a brief nod as he entered the dining room. Cledo growled in the direction of the imposter, and Pettic now realised that the dog could sense, probably by smell, that this was not his friend.

After dinner, as they retired to the Great Hall for the concert, Pettic noticed Torren was no longer with the royal party. The queen turned to him and asked if he knew where her son was. Of course, Pettic did not and he bowed to Queen Phillida and apologised for his friend, telling her he thought he may be along in a few moments.

The prince did not appear, neither did the young lady. Pettic worried a little about the non-appearance of both of them. He knew the real Torren would never compromise a young lady, especially one of the nobility, but this was not the real prince and he had no idea what this person would do, so he worried.

It was two days before he managed to see Princess Lucenra alone. They met walking along the corridor near her apartment and she asked him to come with her. They entered her drawing room, and immediately she asked him what he had found out.

'I followed Torren into the woods,' he told her. 'There he met a man. I can't say much about him because he was all muffled up in cloaks and scarves. He did, however, greet Torren by the name of Dilrong. He did a spell on his ring and then said, "*Being Crown Prince, and ultimately King will be well worth it.*"'

Pettic sighed. 'I don't pretend to understand what it was all about, but it seems obvious the person we're seeing as Torren is, in fact, an imposter made to look like him by sorcery.'

The princess looked into Pettic's blue eyes and her brown ones looked worried.

'I think you're right in this, Pettic,' she responded. 'I think it's time we went back to see Blundo, don't you?'

She ran her fingers through her brunette hair and she sat down. 'If what you say is true, then we must find Torren and expose this pretender. We must also find out who the magician is. Is this Dilrong in charge or does the magician want to gain power through him? Too many questions need answering and we need to think hard. Blundo will help us in this, I know. He always liked Torren the best of all of us, I think, and will want to help free him.' She paused and looked up at Pettic. Then she said, almost whispering, 'If he's still alive, that is. This man could have killed him.'

'I'd had that thought too, Lucenra,' replied Pettic, equally quietly, 'but I refuse to even think about that yet.'

'By the way,' the princess brightened a bit, 'Father gave Torren a severe dressing down for missing the concert the other night. He told him it was very rude of him, and he wouldn't have expected him to act in that way. Of course, the real Torren would never have done so even if he didn't like the music.'

'I think he was with that girl, you know, the daughter of the Duke of Kroldor. He managed to wangle a seat next to her at dinner, and she didn't appear at the concert either.'

'Oh, no! I hope that he hasn't compromised her virtue. Torren would never have done so, of course, but this Dilrong? Who knows?'

The pair left the room and went to find Blundo. Unfortunately he was not in his tower, and his assistant had no idea as to his whereabouts so they left a message. They both returned to their own apartments to wait for a note saying Blundo had returned and could see them.

Cledo was delighted to see his master return and he jumped around like a puppy until Pettic laughingly told him to go and lie down. Just then, the door opened and there stood Torren.

'I've decided I've been neglecting you,' he told Pettic as he entered uninvited and sat down on one of the chairs. 'I think we should have a game of cards. Get yours out. I didn't bring mine.'

Pettic had to remind himself that this was not the prince. Torren would never have entered uninvited, nor spoken to him like that. Pettic felt like a servant and not a friend. Still, he bit his tongue and went to get his cards.

Cledo began growling again as soon as Torren entered and Pettic thrust the dog unceremoniously into his bedroom. When he came back with the cards, Torren had arranged the card table in the centre of the room and placed four chairs round it.

'Are we expecting someone else?' queried Pettic. Torren had said nothing about anyone else coming.

'Yes,' replied the other. 'It's always more fun with four. I've invited that pretty daughter of the Duke of Kroldor and her friend to join us.' He laughed. 'I think the girl likes me—what's her name—I must remember before she arrives. Oh yes. Zoila. I'm hoping I can get to know her *much* better.' Here he winked at Pettic.

'*Oh dear*,' thought Pettic. '*I think he may be thinking about, how did Lucenra put it? "Compromising her virtue."*'

The girls arrived, obviously flattered to be asked to play cards with the Crown Prince. They giggled as they entered Pettic's apartment and sat down around the table. Pettic asked what game the girls would like to play and then Zoila took the cards and shuffled them before dealing them out to the others.

Half way through the game, in which Torren insisted they play for real money, a knock sounded on the door. Pettic excused himself and went to answer it. It was Lucenra.

'I've just had a note to say that Blundo's back and can see us whenever we want,' she said.

The voice of Torren came from behind . 'What do you want to see Blundo about?' he demanded.

'Oh, Torren,' Lucenra said, 'I didn't know you were here.' She thought quickly and said, 'Pettic and I have been having an argument about magic, what it can and can't do, you know? We went to see Blundo to ask which of us is right.'

'Oh, is that all. I wondered if one of you were thinking about taking it up. A bit old though, both of you. I believe you have to start very young and what's more, have an aptitude for it. Anyway, Pettic can't come with you now. We're in the middle of a game and I'm winning.'

Pettic shrugged and mouthed 'Sorry' to the princess. Then he said aloud, 'Why don't you go and see Blundo? You can tell me what he says about our problem and let me know. I promise I'll believe every word you say, even if you tell me he said I'm wrong.'

With that, he closed the door as the princess walked despondently away and he turned back to the game.

'I know,' laughed Torren, 'Why don't we have a game of strip poker?'

The two girls looked worried.

'I don't know how to play poker,' said Zoila.

'Don't worry,' the prince reassured her, 'It's easy. You'll pick it up in no time.'

'I'm not sure about this, Torren,' Pettic said. 'The girls haven't played before and are certain to lose.'

Torren grinned and winked at Pettic, mouthing 'Of course, that's the idea.' Then he said aloud, 'Come on, it'll be great. Just a bit of harmless fun. What's wrong with that?'

The other three continued to argue until Torren lost his temper.

'I'm the Crown Prince. I'll be your king some day. You will obey me. I want to play strip poker, so we'll play strip poker!'

With a sigh they gave in and played the game. Soon the girls were down to their undergarments and nearly crying. Torren called for another hand. He was still fully dressed and Pettic had only lost his jacket and shirt.

'No more, Torren,' said Pettic. 'Can't you see the girls are upset?'

'Oh, tosh. They're only pretending. They're enjoying showing off their bodies. All females enjoy being looked at and admired, and how I'm admiring these two!'

At this point, Zoila's friend stood up and gathered her clothes.

'Crown Prince or not, my future monarch or not, I'm not playing any more. I'm going to put my clothes back on and so is Zoila and we're leaving. I cannot believe that the man we were told is so honourable and gallant would do this to us.'

She strode off, pulling Zoila with her into the bedroom.

As soon as she opened the door, a grey streak shot past her and leaped on Torren snarling. Pettic dragged the dog off and sent him back to the bedroom while picking up the prince.

'That animal is dangerous. I'll have one of the guards sent up here to put him down. In the meantime, he mustn't be allowed out of your quarters. If I see him around the palace, I'll have you banished.'

Torren strode out of the room, leaving two crying girls and a very angry Pettic.

It was much later in the day that Pettic and Lucenra managed to get to see the court magician. Pettic had been much upset by the threat to his dog, even though he knew intellectually this was not the prince, the imposter was so like him it was hard to put it into context. He was also annoyed and upset by the treatment of the two girls.

He spent a lot of time talking to Lucenra about the earlier events and then a few hours in the stables finding someone to look after his dog, somewhere away from the palace. One of the stable hands agreed in the end and Pettic smuggled the animal out and the lad led the reluctant wolfhound away to his home. The dog had whined as the stablehand led him away, making Pettic feel guilty.

The time arrived to visit the magician in his tower. Pettic and Lucenra climbed the stairs quickly and knocked on the door to Blundo's rooms. They entered when the magician called out to them.

'Sorry we're late,' Lucenra said. 'We were caught up in something. Actually, it has to do with Torren. His behaviour is becoming more bizarre and unpleasant. But first Pettic must tell you what he's found out.'

Pettic began his tale and told about how he had followed Torren to his meeting with the mysterious magician in the woods and what he heard and saw.

Blundo rubbed his chin, thinking, and then said, 'It sounds very much as if what you suspect is true. What you saw, is a remaking of the spell on the gem that holds the illusion true. It seems Prince Torren has indeed been abducted or killed and an impostor put in his place. I sincerely hope he hasn't been killed. We must assume he's imprisoned somewhere and work on that premise.'

Lucenra thought for a few minutes and then said, 'Perhaps if we followed the impostor again when he goes off by himself we can find out something about where the real Torren's imprisoned. We can then tell father and he can send troops to rescue him.'

'Woah there,' cried Pettic. 'What do you mean by 'We'? It might be dangerous and if Torren is dead, which heaven forbid, then you're the heir to the throne. You can't be put in danger!'

'Torren *isn't* dead,' the princess retorted. 'I can feel it deep down inside. Anyway, there may be times when you can't follow him. I can go then.'

'What about recruiting the younger princess and princes? Could they help?' suggested Blundo.

Both Pettic and Lucenra cried out together. 'No, It's too dangerous.'

'No doubt they'd like to get involved,' Lucenra went on, 'but it's not going to happen. They must know as little of this as possible. Nothing if I have my way. They're all too impulsive and would no doubt put themselves at risk trying to solve a mystery.'

'Just a thought,' Blundo apologised.

They left it at that. Blundo was to do more research and he would also try to find out about any magicians who had recently moved into the area. Lucenra and Pettic would continue to follow Torren whenever they could.

Sitting in his apartment in the palace, Pettic thought about the past few months and tried to decide exactly when Torren had started behaving oddly. It was, he decided, after he had been crowned as Crown Prince. This always took place on the eighteenth birthday of the heir to the throne and gave him some more responsibility. He or she was gradually taught how a monarch should govern. Torren had been excited at this and about being able to take some of the responsibilities of the crown.

On the day of the birthday that the two friends shared, the coronation of the Crown Prince took place followed by a formal dinner. Pettic got dressed in his best, and made his way to the chapel where the Archbishop was to perform the ceremony.

He expected to be seated at the back, as a commoner, but to his surprise the usher guided him to a seat just behind the Royal

Family. He queried this and the usher told him Prince Torren himself had insisted Pettic be seated there. He told the organisers Pettic was his best friend and he would not countenance him being anywhere but near the Royal Family. He had, after all, been brought up in the royal nurseries and was like a brother to Torren.

After the coronation, Prince Torren stepped forward to take the oath, which he did in a strong voice. Then, against all precedent, he stepped forward and called Pettic to come up. Pettic looked around, surprised, but the king waved him to do as Torren said, and so Pettic stood and slowly walked up to the prince.

The prince turned his friend to face the crowd of people in the royal chapel. He then announced to them all that, with the agreement of the King, his first act as Crown Prince was to endow his best friend with a title. The Earl of Flindon had recently died without any heirs. As he was the last in line to that earldom, Prince Torren had asked the king if his friend could take on the role. His father readily agreed and Pettic had been duly crowned with the small coronet that made him an Earl. Torren was himself at this point. The false Torren would never have thought of this, Pettic was sure.

Three days after their visit to Blundo, the two young people had not needed to follow Torren, as he had not gone off alone. The prince kept to his rooms or went out and about with some new friends from the guards. He seemed to have forgotten about his threat to Cledo, but Pettic did not dare to bring the animal back to the palace because of the dog's perpetual growling whenever Torren appeared. This would no doubt remind the prince of his threat, and probably get Pettic banished from the palace, if not the capital, for disobedience.

The day for the next meeting with Blundo arrived and Lucenra and Pettic met on the way to the magician's tower quarters. ('Why do magicians always live in towers?' Pettic asked one day, but no one seemed to know the answer to that question.)

On the way they met Torren.

'You two seem to be spending a lot of time together these days,' he said, scowling. He turned to Pettic. 'I hope you don't have designs on my sister. She's a princess, you know, and can't possibly marry a commoner, so forget it.'

The princess looked at her brother, eyes flashing.

'Pettic's not a commoner. Remember, you yourself raised him to an earldom. This makes him part of the nobility.'

'He was born a commoner, and will remain a commoner no matter what titles we give him. Nobility comes with birth,' he sneered.

With that, he strode away down the corridor leaving the pair staring after him in amazement.

When they arrived at Blundo's quarters, they found him in a state of excitement. He had found something exciting among the papers left by his predecessor, he told them.

'It was a book about different planes of existence,' he said. 'It seems that there are four other planes besides this one corresponding to the four elements, Earth, Air, Fire and Water. This plane is a combination of all four. I suppose that's why our world is called Fusionem. A fusion of all the other planes. There are ways of passing between these planes if you know how.'

'What's this got to do with Torren?' Pettic asked.

'Ah! I've not finished. Have patience young man. I also found a diary. It was my predecessor's diary.'

He turned to Lucenra. 'I believe your father banished my predecessor. Am I right?'

'Yes, for treason. Father found he'd been in touch with some people who were plotting to overthrow him.'

She gave a little laugh. 'He denied taking part in the conspiracy, of course, saying he didn't know why these people wanted the spells he prepared for them. Father was reluctant to take action against him because he'd been with us for a great many years and had become a friend. However, Father decided he had to banish him just in case. Father said that he should have found out what the spells were for in any case, if he were innocent.'

'That explains why he seemed so bitter in his diary. He must have forgotten to take it when he left. He'd hidden it though, behind some other books. In it he rails about his banishment and says he'll get his revenge somehow.'

Blundo picked up some books on the table in front of him. 'Later on, he says he's found a way to pass to other planes. He mentioned these books. I looked at them and I think I know what's happened.'

The two young people leaned forward expectantly as Blundo paused for dramatic emphasis.

'Go on,' Pettic urged.

'Well, these books say it's possible to pass to another realm by walking through the arches in the Standing Stones outside the city. The moon must be shining through, and be full. Then you pass through to one of the other realms.'

'So you think that Torren's in one of these other planes?' said the princess.

'No. What I read leads me to think that Prince Torren is imprisoned in what Hellom (that was his name, wasn't it?) in what Hellom called a mini-plane, or a 'Bubble'. It's one created by a magician for his or her own purpose. Hellom wrote at length about creating one. I think he's put the prince in that mini-plane.'

'So what's all this about the other realms then?' Pettic asked. We just need to find out how to get into this 'Bubble' and get Torren out.'

'Ah, it's not so simple. There are four keys created by Hellom and he's hidden one in each of the elemental realms. Anyone wanting to enter the Bubble needs all of the keys.' He opened one of the books at a page he had marked. 'They are all precious stones relating to the elements and set in some kind of artefact. The one relating to Terra, the realm corresponding to the element of Earth, is an emerald. Aeris, or Air is a diamond, Aqua which is the water elemental realm, a sapphire and Ignis, or fire, is a ruby.' He closed the book and put it down on the table.

'Unfortunately, we don't know what they're set in. Equally unfortunately, whoever goes to search cannot return without them. They are the keys to the return just as the moon is the key to getting there. Further, although it's the gems that are enchanted, for some reason they will not work to enter the Bubble unless they're in the artefact and worn by the person trying to enter.'

The pair looked at each other.

'It'll need a brave person to take this task on. Whoever goes might not return if they can't find the artefact with the gem in it,' Lucenra said.

'I know,' replied Pettic. 'Since we're the only ones who know about this, and obviously you can't go, it seems it must be me.'

They argued a bit about this, but eventually Lucenra realised that if she disappeared, her parents would be asking questions, and so they agreed Pettic would go.

'There is one more thing,' said Blundo. 'People there in those other worlds will speak a different language. I can make an amulet that'll allow you to understand others and them to understand you. It won't be ready for a couple of days though. I'll send for you as soon as I've got it ready.'

The pair left Blundo then and went to wait impatiently for his summons.

Three days later, Blundo's assistant knocked on Pettic's door. He told him the amulet was ready and he could pick it up as soon as he wished. Blundo also sent a message saying the moon would be full and shining through the arch at six minutes after midnight in two days' time. After that, the next chance would be a full month later.

Pettic decided he was as ready as he would ever be. He admitted to being a little afraid. No one knew what lay beyond the arch—not even what world he would be going to. What if he could not get back? What if it were the world of the element of fire and it was just that—fire and nothing else. Or even water, come to that. He could not breathe if there were no land. Still, he had taken on this task to help to rescue his friend and he would see it through.

He made sure he had enough provisions, although how much was enough? He had no idea how long it would take him to locate the artefact with the gem. He sharpened his sword and stacked a large number of arrows in his quiver. He mentally offered thanks to Torren that he had insisted Pettic learned the arts of weaponry with him. At least he would be able to defend himself from any hostile natives, and maybe even hunt some food if necessary. When he thought he had everything he could think of, he went to see Lucenra.

The princess was ready to go to visit the magician when Pettic knocked at her door, and they left immediately.

When the pair entered his room, Blundo went to a cabinet and unlocked it. He reached in and took out a wooden box, also locked, and lifted a beautiful pendant from it.

'This opal in the amulet has been imbued with the magic for you to understand and be understood,' he said, handing it to Pettic.

The young man slipped it over his head.

'I have something else too,' continued Blundo. 'You'll need to know the gem when you see it, so I've made this little amethyst earring for you. It's fairly unobtrusive but it'll warm when it gets near something magical. The gems will have been imbued with magic, you see, so they can act as keys. Remember, if you get near an emerald, ruby, sapphire or diamond and this warms, it's very likely the gem we want.'

Pettic put the earring in his ear. Lucenra smiled. It made him look quite fetching.

'One more thing.' Blundo continued to speak. 'Time doesn't flow at the same rate in these other worlds, I've been told. It might be quicker or slower, so you may find much time, or no time at all, has passed when you return.

Pettic frowned at this thought, but resolved to continue regardless, even if he found that he had come back here after many years. He still needed to rescue the Crown Prince so he could take his rightful place on the throne when his father died. It was inconceivable this usurper become king. Even more so since the people would not know he was a usurper and would think their beloved Torren had changed into a tyrant. Pettic had no illusions that Dilrong would be anything other than a tyrant.

Chapter 3

Two days later, at ten o' clock in the evening, Lucenra knocked at Pettic's door. The young man was ready, dressed in leather armour for lightness, with his sword at his side and backpack on his back. He had tied his bow to his backpack along with his arrows. His eyes opened wide to see Lucenra standing there in a pair of her brother's trousers and a shirt.

'You aren't planning on coming after all, are you?' demanded Pettic.

'No, but I'm coming to the standing stones with you. I think you should go and get Cledo. He'll help to protect you and give you some companionship too. You'll be all alone there.'

'Good idea, Luce,' replied the young man. 'We've time to go and get him now and still get to the stones in time. Thank you for coming with me.'

The pair crept out of the palace and along the road to where the stable boy who was looking after Cledo lived. Pettic knocked on the door and a loud barking came from inside. The door opened a crack and the boy's father peeped round. A grey flash knocked him unceremoniously aside as Cledo came bounding out to greet Pettic. The young man was nearly felled by the exuberance of his dog.

'Steady, boy,' Pettic told the animal, 'Get down please.' This last as the dog placed his paws on his master's shoulders and began to lick his face. Then he turned to the family standing looking on in awe at the Crown Prince's friend and his sister who were in their cottage.

'Thank you so much for looking after Cledo for me,' he said. 'I'm going away for a little while. I'm not sure how long I'll be so I'm taking Cledo with me. Here's something for your trouble and the expense you incurred in looking after him.'

He handed over a pouch of gold coins—much more than it would have cost them for the dog's keep.

At first the stable boy's father refused, saying it was a pleasure, and what a good dog he was, but Pettic insisted. He, Lucenra and Cledo then went on their way, leaving the family wondering if they were witnesses to an elopement.

It took a while for the three to pass through the town and up onto the little hill where the standing stones were situated. The stones had been there for centuries and no one knew what their original purpose had been. Many rumours grew up around them over the intervening years, though, and many believed them to be haunted.

Pettic now remembered hearing a rumour a long time ago that they were a gateway to other lands. He smiled to himself remembering how he had dismissed that idea as the most preposterous of all of them. How wrong he had been.

Eventually they reached the top of the hill. It was a clear night and the moon threw its dim light across the land. As it climbed higher, the light came nearer and nearer to the arch and Pettic became more nervous, as did Lucenra.

Just as Blundo had said, at six minutes past midnight the first rays of light passed through the arch. Both young people peered through, perhaps hoping to see something of the land beyond, but all they saw was the city spread out below them.

'This is it then,' said Pettic, still looking at the light now streaming through the arch. 'I'd better go before the moon goes and the light no longer passes through the arch.' He turned to the princess. 'Take care of yourself and the others, and try to see if you can control Torren a bit.'

'Not much chance of that, I don't think,' the girl replied. 'Take care of yourself and come back.' She stood on her toes and pecked him on the cheek. 'Now go quickly or you'll be too late.'

She stood and watched as Pettic walked through the arch and disappeared as if going into a mist. She walked slowly down the hill wondering if she would ever see him again, and if his quest would be successful.

Pettic felt no sensation as he walked through the arch, but a mist engulfed him and his dog. It quickly dissipated and they emerged into a cave.

Pettic looked around him and saw that the cave seemed to be a narrow crack in the rock. He had no choice but to follow it as the wall behind him was now solid. The passage quickly opened out into a large chamber.

Stalactites hung from the ceiling and stalagmites climbed from the ground. Some had joined into columns giving the cave a cathedral-like feel.

Then he noticed the people. They surrounded a large flat stone with a goat on it. A dark-skinned man had just cut its throat if the bloody knife he held was anything to go by. The people were kneeling down and chanting. This was obviously some religious ceremony.

Pettic did not want to disturb them. People often became quite angry if anyone disrupted their religious ceremonies so he tried to slink out past them.

Then the man with the knife, who seemed to be leading the ceremony, spotted Pettic and he cried out.

'Look,' he called. 'Our prayers have been answered. Here is Jintor himself with his hound, Oro, come to save us. Praise be to Holy Jintor.' He got down onto his knees and bowed down to Pettic and all the other people did the same.

'Hang on a minute,' said Pettic. 'I think you've got this wrong. I'm not Jintor. My name's Pettic and this is my dog, Cledo.'

'If you wish to be known as 'Pettic', Your Holiness, then so be it, but I saw you come out of the wall in a mist. There is no way out or in to the Holy Cave that way. You must be the god himself. Holy Jintor always travels with his hound, so that is how I knew you. You'll come with us to see our chief?'

Pettic decided he had little choice in the matter. That was the only way out of the cave it seemed. As a god, he supposed, he could pull rank and insist on going his own way, but as he had no idea where he was nor what he faced here, he decided it would be wise to go along with these people, but he would not pretend to be a god. That way lay disaster. Gods were not well known for their tolerance of impostors.

A little procession formed with Pettic and Cledo at its centre. They wanted to carry him, but protestations from Pettic, and a growl or two from Cledo soon got them to agree to allow him to walk.

The procession left the cave and began to walk slowly down a muddy path. A cliff rose up on one side and a dense forest grew on the other. Pettic could hear a stream flowing somewhere ahead and soon they passed a waterfall cascading down the cliff. The stream then continued on its way alongside the path.

Eventually they reached a village surrounded by a palisade made of sharpened stakes. The people led Pettic through a gate in the palisade. The village comprised many round huts with thatched roofs scattered around in what seemed like a random fashion. None were very far from the stream that had turned away from the cliff and flowed towards a lake in the valley below.

Villagers ran out to see what was happening. The people accompanying them, along with the priests, made their way to a much larger hut at the far end of the village.

Once there, the chief priest, the one with the knife, banged on a drum he carried and an imposing man came out from the large hut. He looked to be around forty five years old and was dressed in a white robe that contrasted with his dark skin and hair. His nose was straight and his mouth wide and generous but he had a look of sadness in his brown eyes. He spoke to the chief priest.

'Who is this man? Where did he come from?'

'We were praying for aid when this man and his dog came through in a mist from the dead-end passage at the back of the Holy Cave. He can only be a god. Since he has all the accoutrements of Holy Jintor and his hound Oro, we assumed it was the god himself. However, he says he's not the god, but a man called Pettic. We brought him to you immediately.'

The tall man beckoned to Pettic to step forward. As he did so the priest and his followers stepped back. The tall man looked Pettic in the eyes and then turned, and beckoning him to follow, returned to the hut.

Pettic followed and entered past a curtain of beads rather than a door and found himself in a dim room. The hut had no windows so it was rather dark, the only light coming through the doorway, where a tie held the curtain back.

When his eyes became accustomed, he noticed mats on the floor with a woman sitting on one of them. She appeared to be a few years younger than the headman, for this man was undoubtedly the leader of this community. Pettic assumed she was his wife.

The headman bade him sit and went to another mat where he, too, sat.

'Now, tell me who you are. Are you the god, Jintor with his hound Oro? It would seem you must be because of the way you appeared here on Terra. There's no other way into the Holy Cave other than the main entrance, yet my chief priest tells me that you came from the little passage at the back.

He smiled. 'This means you're either what he said, the god Jintor, or an impostor who somehow got into the cave before my priests went in. Since there have been people in there praying for help for the last seven sunrises and there's no food and water in there, if you're not Jintor, then it's a mystery.'

'I'm not your god,' replied Pettic carefully, 'nor is my dog the hound, Oro, of whom you speak. I'm just a man, but have come here by magical means. I passed through an arch in some standing stones in my world when the full moon was shining through. I went into a mist and ended up in the cave passage you describe. My name's Pettic and I'm here because the Crown Prince of my country is in grave danger and there's something here I need in order to rescue him.'

'Yet you've all the accoutrements of Jintor. You have a grey hound, a sword at your hip and a bow slung across your back. You've white-fletched arrows, your hair and skin are fair and your eyes are blue. Fair skin and blue eyes aren't known in this world. My priests have been praying for aid for many long sunrises and the hunter god would be just the one we need. Perhaps if you aren't he, then he's sent you?'

'Why do you need aid?'

The headman sighed.

'There's a large, nay, gigantic phantom boar that's been attacking my people and their animals. Everyone who's gone up against it has been killed. We need a seasoned hunter—one who's fearless and indestructible—to rid us of this phantom. It seems the gods have sent you and your animal to aid us.'

Pettic shuddered. A phantom boar? That he did not believe. He could believe there was a large animal out there but he had never put much credit in tales of ghosts. He wondered why people said it was a phantom and he asked the headman.

'It's all white and appears at night. Boars are creatures of the sun but this one shuns the day. You, a great hunter, must go out and kill this menace to my people. Only last week he killed my eldest son. He thought himself great enough to kill it, but he wasn't.'

A tear escaped from the headman's eye. He allowed it to roll down his cheek. His wife, on hearing the mention of their son began to wail. The headman got up and went to comfort her, calling back to Pettic that he may leave.

When Pettic left the headman's hut he found the whole village gathered together waiting for him. As he emerged, they all fell to their knees and began to chant as one, praising him as Holy Jintor. Pettic raised his hand and told them to stop, that he was not their god.

A silence fell and the Chief Priest stood and said, 'We obey you, Holy Lord. If you wish to be known as Pettic and Cledo, then so shall it be. We, however know who you are truly by your face, hair and eyes. Only the gods are so fair.'

Pettic sighed and resigned himself to the situation. At least he had got them to stop treating him with such reverence. (At least he thought he had.) He stood looking round as the people got to their feet and wandered away and the priest came to speak with him.

'I'll escort you to the guest hut, Ho...Pettic,' he said. 'If you care to follow me.'

The pair, followed closely by Cledo and many pairs of eyes, made their way across the open area in front of the headman's hut to another hut on the right hand side of the area. Here stood a hut a little bigger than most of the others. The priest pushed aside the bead curtain and entered, followed by Pettic and Cledo.

Inside it was similar to the headman's hut—dark, but with rush mats on the floor instead of the more comfortable woolen ones he had seen in the headman's hut. He supposed there had to be some perks to being the chief man in the village.

The priest, who said his name was Woller, led Pettic round a curtain dividing the hut into two. A raised platform with a mattress on it dominated the space, with a small, low table next to it. Woller pointed out that this was the sleeping area.

Pettic smiled and thanked him. He said he would like to ask a few questions as he did not know anything about this world. In return, he would answer any questions Woller wanted to ask him.

The two returned to the living area and sat down cross legged on the mats.

'First, I'd like to know where I am. Your headman called this world Terra. I'm looking for a gem set in an artefact. If this is Terra, then I'm looking for an emerald. Have you heard of any such thing?'

Woller thought for a minute then replied, 'Do you have any idea what this artefact is?'

'No, unfortunately. Just that there's some magic on the emerald.'

Woller laughed. 'Magic?' he said. 'How old are you? Only little children believe in magic! Pettic, it doesn't exist.'

'Well, there's magic where I come from. I got here by magic, and we can only understand each other because of an amulet with an opal imbued with magic. Look, I'll take the amulet off and see what happens.'

He lifted the amulet over his head and continued to talk. He saw Woller's face take on a puzzled look.

The other man said, 'Ron droh brew nittrol? Tri frenthy miff scullen ma crynjug.'

Pettic replaced the amulet and said, 'I couldn't understand a word you said then and I don't suppose you understood me, either. The magic on this gem enables us to understand each other.'

Woller looked puzzled. 'How does it work?' he asked.

'No idea.' Pettic told him. 'I'm not a magician. A magician in my world made it.'

'Yet it works for you?'

'Yes.'

'There's no magic on Terra, yet I have to believe you. Only by magic can we understand each other. If you're not a god, (and I'm not truly convinced you're not), then only magic can have brought you here. Do you have magic items that can defeat the phantom boar?'

'No. Only my sword and bow. And my dog, of course. He's a hound and will fight wild beasts.'

Woller stood up. I'll let you rest now. If, as you say, you left your world at night, then you'll be tired. Rest and we'll speak again. I expect the headman will want to see you again as well.'

When Woller left, Pettic stood up and stretched. He yawned. He was tired and so, calling to Cledo, he passed through the curtain and into the sleeping quarters where he slept deeply until dawn the next day.

Chapter 4

In the morning, Pettic woke to hear the sounds of the village coming awake. A cockerel crowed somewhere to the north, where he had entered the village. He heard the rattle of plates and the laughter of children as people prepared the first meal of the day.

He sat up and rubbed his eyes before dressing and going through to the living area of the hut. He found someone had been in and left water and a crude type of soap for him to wash. He rummaged in his pack until he found a razor and washed and shaved himself.

Just as he was finishing and towelling himself dry, someone rattled the bead curtain at the entrance. He assumed this was a request to enter and called out to the person to come in.

The curtain parted and a very pretty girl entered carrying a tray laden with unleavened bread and cheese as well as some kind of cured meat and a hot beverage. She smiled at Pettic as she set the tray down on a low table.

'I've brought you something to eat,' she said. 'My father would like to see you as soon as you're ready. He's the head-man,' she added, seeing Pettic's puzzled expression.

'Thank you…er…I don't know your name,' said Pettic
She smiled and it lit up her face.
'Rolinda,' she replied. 'My name's Rolinda.'

'Well, thank you Rolinda for bringing me this food. I'm really quite hungry now you mention it, but even so I can't possible eat all this food. Would you care to join me?'

'I've already eaten,' replied the girl, 'and although I'd like to join you, I've my tasks to perform. My father would be angry with me if I dallied here with you.'

With that, she left the hut, bowing as she departed.

'Well, Cledo,' Pettic said to his dog, 'it looks like you're going to have to help me eat this. I'm sure you won't find that a difficult task though.'

The dog looked up at his master and wagged his tail at the thought of eating some of the meat he could smell on the tray. Pettic picked up a couple of slices and tossed them down onto the ground where the wolfhound gobbled them up and then sat looking for more.

After eating, Pettic and Cledo left the hut and crossed to the headman's hut. They found the headman sitting on the veranda that ran around the front and sides of the hut. He beckoned the pair over as he saw them crossing what Pettic had come to think of as the Square and they climbed the three steps onto the veranda. As he climbed the last step, Pettic stumbled and nearly fell. The big man laughed a hearty laugh.

'Well, that's a bit clumsy for a god,' he said. 'I really don't think a god would fall in front of people. Perhaps you really aren't Jintor. I think you've convinced Waller. He told me you've magic on your world and we're only understanding each other because of a magic gem in the amulet you're wearing. He also said you came here by magic, but not why you came. At least not in any meaningful detail. You mentioned a "Crown Prince". What's that?'

Pettic went on to tell Borrin, for that was the headman's name, about how he and princess Lucenra became suspicious someone had kidnapped Prince Torren and put an imposter in

34

his place. He told all that had happened and how the prince could be rescued.

After listening intently, the headman thought for a moment and then he spoke.

'There's another tribe across the other side of the lake,' he told Pettic. 'I believe their headman has a sword with an emerald in its pommel. He said he found it hidden in a cave. Perhaps this is the emerald and perhaps not, but I've a proposition to put to you. You get rid of this phantom boar and I'll help you to get the sword with the emerald.'

Pettic thought he had no choice. Emeralds could not be common, even on this world, and so he agreed.

'I'll need to know a lot more about this boar though, like where its lair is, how large it really is, why people think it's a phantom, how many people it's killed and how often, who has been to fight it and what weapons they used. Lots of questions like that.'

They talked for quite some time until Rolinda came out with cold fruit juice for them to drink. By now it was beginning to get hot and Pettic was roasting in his leather armour. Rolinda spotted he was sweating and turned to whisper in her father's ear. He smiled at her and patted her cheek.

'My Rolinda says she thinks you'd be cooler in some robes like the ones we wear. She's a good girl and observant. She's right. I'll have some robes sent over to you so you can be more comfortable.'

Pettic was going to refuse at first but he decided it was the better option. He would certainly to roast in his leather.

He and Borrin continued to talk about their various worlds until the sun was high in the sky, then Borrin told Pettic that at this time the people retired to their huts to rest during the hottest part of the day. Pettic had noticed the Square emptying and wondered why. He gratefully left Borrin's hut and returned to his own.

On entering the hut he realised why there were no windows. It was comparatively cool inside and when he passed through the curtain to rest, he found white robes laid out on the bed.

He gratefully removed his armour but decided he would wait until later to don the robes. He collapsed onto the bed. Cledo jumped up and snuggled up beside him. Pettic pushed the dog away as he was already hot and the proximity of the animal made him hotter. Cledo whined, but moved to the edge of the bed.

Pettic did not intend to sleep. He had slept so long the previous night he thought he would be unable to do so. He resolved to think about everything he had learned about this world and the sword with the emerald but he soon found himself drifting off.

When he woke up it was late afternoon. He dressed in the robe and, feeling much cooler, left his hut. The village was busy again with people coming out now the sun was lower in the sky.

Many of the folk seemed to be going in the direction of the lake, and Pettic followed. Once there the people picked up a variety of tools and began to hoe the ground between rows of vegetables.

The crops grew behind fences and the reason for this soon became evident when a small herd of pigs came out of the forest. They began to forage around the field and would undoubtedly have uprooted the crops if they could get in.

He entered the field and picked up a hoe. This was something he understood. Working on a farm. He had been brought up on a farm until the age of thirteen when he became the friend and companion of Torren. After the proclamation had gone out inviting boys who were thirteen on the same day as the prince, his parents took him and his little brother, Derkil, to Glitton. They went to the palace along with a crowd of others, mainly nobility.

Before their interview, Pettic went to visit the garderobe. On the way back he got lost in the corridors of the palace. where he met a young boy of about his age and asked him where he should go to get back to the Great Hall.

The boy was very helpful. Pettic asked him if he worked at the palace.

The boy replied, 'You could say that, I suppose.'

They talked on their way back to the great hall. The boy was fascinated to hear about Pettic's life. He told Pettic he did not know anything about life on a farm because he had lived all his life in the palace. Pettic chatted on about his family and told the boy about some of his escapades, which made the boy laugh.

Eventually they arrived back at the hall, and the boy rushed off saying he was late for an appointment.

Imagine Pettic's surprise when he went into the King's office and found the boy sitting next to the king. It was Prince Torren himself who had escorted him back to the hall.

The prince insisted Pettic was the boy he wanted to be his companion. King Horaic II tried to persuade his son that perhaps a noble boy would be a better choice, but Torren and Pettic hit it off so well that the prince insisted. The king told him he would have free choice in who to employ and so Pettic got the job of companion to the Crown Prince.

In the intervening years, although he returned to the farm for visits and even took Torren on occasions, he missed working on the land. He joined in with the villagers with gusto, much to their surprise.

They worked until the sun was setting. Pettic looked at his lovely, cool, white robe. It was no longer white but spattered with mud from the fields. One of the villagers assured him if he left it outside his hut someone would come to take it and wash it. Another would be provided in the meantime.

Seeing the headman and his family working alongside the villagers also surprised him. The only people who were not helping were the small children and those women who were preparing the evening meal.

As the sun sank below the horizon, everyone picked up the tools and wended their way back to the village where the women had prepared a meal.

The people all sat on straw mats in the centre of the village and ate from carved wooden bowls. The food was delicious. The main meat was pork and it had been cooked long and slow with herbs and spices gathered from the forest.

Pettic felt very hungry after his exertions in the fields and he ate heartily, chatting to various villagers, all of whom were interested in where he came from and how he got there. Magic, especially, interested them and they exclaimed at some of the things Pettic told them.

After eating, Borrin came over and asked Pettic to come to his hut the next morning. Pettic helped the villagers to clear up after the meal and then they all repaired to their huts for the night.

As they did not have much in the way of lighting, just a few oil-based lamps that did not give much light, the people went to bed and rose with the sun. Pettic and Cledo went to their hut, carrying a small lamp. Pettic felt a satisfaction he had not felt for a long time after his efforts in the fields, and he fell into his bed feeling a pleasant tiredness.

The next morning Pettic was awakened by the sounds of someone in his living area.

He jumped out of bed and pulled on his robe. On entering the room he found Rolinda putting a tray of fruit on the low table and also a jug of hot water for him to wash in.

He smiled at her and thanked her before she left through the curtain door. It was still dark, but the sun was coming up over the hills behind the village and already people were busy in the Square. Pettic remembered his promise to go to see Borrin, so he washed quickly and ate the fruit left for him before leaving for the headman's hut.

By the time he arrived, the sun had risen above the hills and it was beginning to get hot in spite of the earliness of the day.

Borrin was sitting on his veranda on the skin of some beast. He called to Pettic when he saw him emerge and beckoned him over.

'I'm glad you aren't late,' he said. 'We must talk about making plans for you to go and rid us of this boar, although if it is a phantom, as many of my people believe, I don't know quite how it's to be done.'

Pettic sat down on a rug next to the headman and said, 'It may not be a phantom, you know. The people think it is because of its colour and the fact that it only seems to be seen at night. Sometimes, very rarely, an all white creature is produced. We call it an albino. They have no pigment in their skin and are very susceptible to sunlight as a result. Perhaps the boar is one of these.'

Pettic rubbed his nose as a fly landed. 'This may be why it's only ever seen at night. As to its size, well, I've no ideas on that score except to say perhaps the descriptions have been exaggerated.'

'Perhaps,' Borrin replied. 'It may be as you say, but time will tell.' He turned to the hut and called out a name. 'Klondor, come out here a moment, will you?'

Someone pushed the bead curtain aside and a young man about the same age as Pettic came through. He was obviously a close relative of the headman by their likeness to each other.

'This is my son, Klondor,' said the headman. 'Woller suggested he accompany you to help you find this creature. You don't know the country round here and he can help you find your way around and show you where the boar has been seen recently. He's also an expert tracker, despite his youth, and good with the bow.'

'Thank you,' replied Pettic. 'I am sure he'll be helpful to me. And another person good with a bow is always useful.'

'He's also accomplished in the use of a spear. A spear is good for hunting animals like the boar as you can stab him from a distance and not be in danger from his tusks.'

'The spear is not a weapon I've had any experience with,' said Pettic. 'I'd be grateful for a partner who can use one.'

The three men sat together on the veranda planning how they would tackle this large animal until they eventually had something of a plan. Borrin, of course was not going to go on the hunt with them, but he offered to send some more young men if the pair thought it would help.

'I really don't think it would, father,' said Klondor. 'Sometimes fewer is better. A large number would probably spook the creature and the more people there are the more likely it is that someone will make a noise and warn the creature of our presence. That could be very dangerous if the boar thought he was under attack and decided to attack in his turn.'

'You're right, of course,' sighed the headman. 'I just didn't want to lose another son and thought there maybe safety in numbers; but I know in some cases that isn't so. Now, tell me more about this Crown Prince you're so keen on rescuing that you're willing to sacrifice your life for him. First of all, what's a Crown Prince?

Pettic began to explain.

'First of all, in my world, the land is divided into countries. They're large areas of land, sometimes whole islands, that are governed together. We don't have villages that are governed autonomously. Each village or town has a mayor who sees to all the local things, but over everyone there's a king who has responsibility for the whole country.'

'Very interesting,' said Borrin, frowning, 'but isn't it difficult for one man to govern so much land and so many people. Goodness, I've enough trouble with the people in my village without adding any more!'

'The king has many people, called "councillors", to advise him. Also, most minor problems and disputes are sorted out by the local mayor, much as I assume you do here.'

'Hmm,' said the headman. 'Now what about this Crown Prince?'

'The king's children are princes and princesses. They'll all have influence in some way. They'll be given titles and places to govern, if only a large castle with land. The eldest child of the king or queen, because a woman can take the throne too, is called the Crown Prince or Princess. He, or she, will become the next king or queen on the death of the current monarch.'

'How very odd,' Borrin responded. 'What if he or she isn't suitable? Perhaps is of feeble mind or of a violent temperament or some such. I find it odd that you give equal credence to the women—that a woman can become, what did you call it? A queen? Here only men can stand for the head of a village and the people choose the most likely candidate. It may be the son of the current headman (I had hopes of my elder son becoming headman after me, but that can't be now, thanks to that boar) or it might be another person. So it's your next ruler you're intent on rescuing. I begin to understand.'

'He's not just my next king, but my best friend, too.'

'Go now with Klondor and get to know each other a bit better before you go on your boar hunt.'

Pettic introduced Klondor to Cledo. The dog seemed to like the other young man and that pleased Pettic. It would have been very difficult if the dog had not liked his companion. The pair strode off across the village square to where a hut stood alone.

'This hut is where we keep our weapons. There are all sorts in there. Many of the arrows have metal tips, and some of the spears, but many are just sharpened and hardened wood. We've a tree that's good for making bows and there are many long bows from this tree. They have a much better range than the short bows, but you know that already.'

The pair entered the hut and looked round. There were windows in this hut although on the north side, as it did not need to be kept cool for living in. Klondor picked a bow and selected some arrows and a long spear. Then the pair left the hut and went to the guest hut where Pettic showed the other young man his own weapons and also his leather armour.

They found they got on very well. They both had a similar sense of humour and by the time the evening meal came around they were firm friends. They sat next to each other and laughed throughout the meal. Their laughter was so infectious that the other villagers found themselves laughing along with the pair. The sun set all too soon and everyone went to their huts and bed.

Borrin decided there should be a feast before the two hunters set off and the next evening was set aside for that. Fewer people went to the fields this day, and some of those who did were collecting vegetables for the feast.

Nearly all the village women were doing something towards the preparations so it was mainly men and children who worked in the fields. Pettic and Klondor went down to work even though they were told there was no need as the feast was in their honour.

The meal began earlier than usual because it was going to be a large meal. Before they began, Woller stood up and praised the gods for the bounty before them, then they began to eat.

A great variety of vegetables, all cooked in different ways, covered the table. Some were familiar to Pettic, but some were not. He enjoyed them all. They had killed a calf for the event and wasted nothing of it.

Borrin carved the meat up as a particular delicacy, but they also served the liver, kidneys and other offal.

There was a kind of spicy sausage in the intestines and the stomach had been stuffed with a mixture of grains and herbs. The head of the calf was boiled and put on a plate and served first to Borrin and his guest. Borrin cut some of the meat from the cheek and then spooned some of the brains onto it. Pettic was not sure about this, but thought he had better overcome his squeamishness in order not to seem rude. To his surprise he actually enjoyed it.

During the meal, instead of the fruit juices and water that had been served with the other meals he had eaten on Terra, or the hot beverage he had at breakfast time, a fermented drink was served. This was quite potent, and soon everyone was in excellent spirits.

As the drink was being served, Woller stood again.

'Before we are all incapable,' he intoned, 'We should pray for these two brave young men who are going out to try to rid us of this menace, the phantom boar. Many other young men have been before, but none have returned. We all know the names of those. I believe that the same goes for other villages as well.' He then raised his hands and began to pray.

'Holy Jintor,' he prayed, 'you who are the greatest huntsman of all, watch over these two young men in their hunt for our nemesis. We pray for the soul of this beast that we call the Phantom Boar. We pray that it is truly a mortal beast and not a phantom as we have named it. We also thank you for sending us Pettic as your emissary. Guide his arrows truly that he may kill this creature. Also for Klondor, our headman's son. May his spear be true and may he come back alive. You saw fit to take the souls of others through this beast, now, we beg of you, let these brave young men succeed where others have failed. We ask this in the name of your father, Golind, and your mother Jani, but not our will be done, but yours.'

He lowered his hands and sat down. Everyone, including Woller, then picked up their bowls and the drinking began.

Chapter 5

The next morning Pettic woke feeling terrible. His head thumped and his stomach recoiled when he thought about food. He was glad the huts had no windows. He knew he would not be able to stand the light. He remembered drinking rather a lot at the feast the previous evening, and he remembered the drumming and then the flutes.

He vaguely remembered dancing, although what kind of dance he did not know. He remembered everyone laughing at him stumbling over the steps. He remembered kissing several of the girls there too, and he thought Rolinda might have been one of them, but was unsure. He hoped his memory of that was wrong. He did not know how her father would take it. Beyond that his memory failed him, and even some of the memories he did have seemed to belong to someone else.

Cledo put his feet on the edge of the bed and began to lick his master's face.

'Get off, Cledo,' Pettic demanded. 'I'm feeling ill. Leave me alone.'

He rolled over away from the dog. Then his stomach recoiled again and he rushed outside and just managed to get through the door before he lost a good proportion of last night's feast.

A rather wobbly Woller approached.

'Feeling bad, are you?' he asked sympathetically. 'I'm not really surprised. Both you and young Klondor had rather a lot to drink. He's behind his hut now, doing exactly the same as you. The boar hunt will need to be postponed for today. I'll make sure there's only fruit juice or water tonight so you'll be fine tomorrow. Anyway, most of the village is in a bad way this morning, myself included. I'll go back to my hut now and lie down in the dark again. I only came out to see how both you boys are.'

As Woller wobbled across the square again, Pettic staggered back into his hut and returned to bed.

When he woke again he felt a little better, but very thirsty. He got up and went to find some water. Quite a lot of people were out and about now, but there no one was working in the fields today.

He managed to find someone to tell him where he could get a drink, and shortly began to feel much better. Klondor came out of the headman's hut and greeted him, if a little gingerly.

'What a time we had last night!' he called.

'I'll believe you,' Pettic replied. 'My memory's a little vague about quite a lot of it. I hope I didn't disgrace myself.'

'Don't worry about that. I'm sure you didn't, but even if you did, no one will remember. There was more drink flowing last night than I can ever remember.'

'One thing's for sure though. We can't start our boar hunt today. I'm not feeling well enough.'

The other young man laughed. 'No more am I, Pettic. We'll leave tomorrow morning though, at dawn.'

'Will your father be angry that we've not gone today as planned?'

'No! He was as drunk as the rest of the village. He knew what would happen and we'd not be going today. In fact, Woller already predicted a start tomorrow would be the best. My father only put it about we were going today so we could get the feast done yesterday. He knew we'd be in no fit state after it.'

'Very clever. I suppose that's one of the reasons he's headman. Being clever.'

'Some might call it underhand. The feast's supposed to take place the evening before a big event. Still, we'll be off tomorrow. I can't wait. It's about time they allowed me to go on an adventure of my own, but ever since my brother was killed, I've been kept close to home. I owe Woller one for saying I should go with you. He said it was the will of Jakim or somesuch.'

The two young men spent the day together talking about everything under the sun. They planned their hunt in detail, discarded the plans, made new ones then came back to the original one. Klondor petted Cledo, who wagged his tail and licked his master's new friend's hand. Then they noticed the villagers getting ready for the evening meal and they repaired to the Square to eat.

That night, Klondor dragged his bed from the headman's hut into the guest hut. They planned to leave early, before the sun and the people rose.

As the sun's first light showed over the hills, the two young men and the wolfhound approached the lake in the valley below. Klondor told Pettic the boar had last been seen in the hills on the opposite side of the lake. They passed another village at the head of the lake. People called out to them and Klondor waved but they did not stop.

They continued round the lake and stopped to have a drink. It was not the habit of the people on this world of Terra to eat in the middle of the day and so they contented themselves with a drink before continuing to a narrow game trail that led down to the shoreline.

From here the trail led up into low hills that gradually climbed up to high mountains. By nightfall they had reached a forest and they set up camp by a small stream.

They had no tent. The temperatures in this part of the world meant sleeping outside was an attractive prospect. The only thing that Klondor insisted on was Pettic douse himself in a liquid made by boiling up some kind of herb in water from the stream. It would keep the biting insects away, Klondor told him.

Pettic did as he was told. He had experience of the discomfort of insect bites on his parents' farm. He had scratched one to try to relieve the itching and it became infected. He had been quite ill from the infection and he did not want to repeat that experience.

During the night, Pettic awoke to feel something crawling up his arm. He looked and saw the biggest spider he had ever seen in his life slowly making its way towards his face. It was black with yellow stripes and looked dangerous. He nearly jumped up but, not knowing if it were poisonous or not, he remained as still as he could. He called out to Klondor. The other young man woke and instantly assessed the situation.

'Don't move!' he told Pettic. 'If you move it may be spooked and bite you. Trust me, you don't want to be on the receiving end of a bite from a tiger spider.'

Pettic remained as still as he could while his friend took a dagger from out of his boot. Then, as quickly as Pettic could think, Klondor had slipped the knife under the creature's belly and flicked if off Pettic's shoulder, for it had reached that far. Then, equally quickly, Klondor threw his knife and speared the spider cleanly as it ran for the cover of the trees. Only then could Pettic begin to breathe again.

'Thanks, Klondor,' he said. 'That was pretty neat.'

'A tiger spider's bite is very nasty. They don't usually kill, they don't have enough poison for that, but they have enough to make you wish they had. I didn't think there were any around here. Seems I was mistaken.' He paused and looked at the sky. 'We could be setting off now. It's still a little time until sunrise, but I don't suppose you'll feel like sleeping again now, and I'm not sure I do after that.'

When the two had packed up their things, they ate a little cheese and bread they had brought with them and set off once more.

After a couple of hours, Klondor told Pettic they were approaching the place where the boar had last been seen and they slowed down. Klondor began to cast around for any signs of the animal.

Soon he found what appeared to be prints of a large cloven-hoofed animal. He deduced this was the creature they were hunting but told Pettic that the tracks were a few days old. They had a drink and gave Cledo one too, before setting off in the direction the tracks took.

The boar had wandered around, backtracking several times. Twice they lost the tracks but soon managed to pick them up again. Once he realised what the men were tracking, Cledo helped by sniffing out tracks they had not noticed.

It was not generally difficult to follow where the animal had been because it stopped at regular intervals to forage leaving turned up soil, but the creature followed such a winding track it took them most of the day before they came to where the creature had its lair.

A cave loomed ahead in the side of a hill. The tracks led into this cave. It was still daylight so there was no sign of the nocturnal animal.

The two young men decided to wait until the creature came out of the cave. Boars have very poor eyesight and so they had few worries about being spotted if they were in the trees. There was plenty of brush around and a small pond lay not far away with evidence of having been used as a wallow for the animal.

Cledo, now scenting boar strongly, began to jump around and Pettic had to use all his authority with the dog to get him to sit calmly and wait.

Shortly, the sun began to set. Pettic and Cledo stayed where they were while Klondor worked his way through the brush to the other side of the cave. When it was almost fully dark Pettic spotted something moving in the cave mouth.

There stood the biggest boar Pettic had ever seen. It was easily the size of a small pony. It was white and its little eyes were pink, confirming Pettic's view that it was an albino. Its head was large, about one third of its body, as is the case with all boars, and it had a large mane of white hair on its shoulders.

Pettic wondered if it had reproduced. An adult male that size would have surely won any fights for females. If this were the case, then perhaps there were other potentially large and dangerous beasts out there.

The boar stood in the entrance and sniffed the air. When it thought it safe, it came out of the cave and trotted off towards the pond where it drank.

An old carcass lay there. Pettic thought it was probably some carrion the boar had been eating. Boars rarely killed large animals even though they were omnivores, preferring to eat small things but this creature was so much bigger than the average boar it may require bigger game. Borrin had certainly told of it killing people, and not just in self-defence.

The sound of a nightjar came from the other side of the cave. Klondor gave this sign to say he was going to attack. Pettic lifted the bow from his back and nocked an arrow. Drawing the string back as far as he could he aimed at the boar.

Saying a silent prayer to Jakim, even though he was not a god of his world, Pettic released the string. The arrow flew true and struck the boar on his shoulder. At the same time a javelin flew at the creature from the other side of the cave. The javelin stuck into the thick muscle on the beast's other shoulder. It gave a scream of pain and turned in a circle not knowing which aggressor to attack first.

'Go, Cledo,' Pettic told the dog and the wolfhound leaped joyfully towards the boar, barking his pleasure.

Hearing the dog, the boar turned towards this more immediate danger. He put down his head to try to injure the dog with his massive tusks. Cledo twisted away and gave Pettic another chance at a shot. This time his arrow went wide.

The boar moved around, trying to have another go at Cledo making the aim difficult. Then Pettic saw Klondor rushing the animal from his hiding place. He had a metal-tipped spear raised to give the killing blow while the boar was distracted by Cledo.

Unfortunately, the boar, having caught Cledo with his tusks threw the whimpering dog aside. He heard the young man and turned to this threat. He charged. Klondor jumped to one side just in time and managed to rip a cut in the boar's hide all down one side. Then he tripped.

With a scream, the boar charged towards Klondor's prostrate form. Pettic could not let his friend be killed as his brother had been. He let another arrow fly. This time he hit the boar again, but did not make a killing blow.

The boar decided the two previous attackers were no immediate threat and turned to Pettic. Pettic thought his red eyes looked evil as he charged. He could not nock another arrow in time so he drew his sword.

The creature came on towards him and time seemed to slow. He knew his death was rushing towards him and he silently apologised to Torren, Lucenra, the king and queen, and his country for failing at the first hurdle.

He raised his sword and just as the animal was about to try to impale him with his tusks, he stepped aside and brought it down, point first, onto the boar's neck. It fell dead at his feet.

He could hardly believe his luck, but before doing anything else, he went over to his friend. Klondor seemed to be unhurt except for a slight cut, not from the boar, but from a branch that he had landed on when he tripped.

Cledo was not so lucky. The dog lay whimpering and a large cut stretched along one side. Pettic knelt down beside his faithful companion and stroked the wolfhound's head. Klondor came up and knelt down by Pettic.

'I have some herbs in my pack I think'll help him,' he said. 'I'll get them.'

He left to get the herbs leaving Pettic with his dog. The young man patted the brave creature and was rewarded with a lick.

'I'm sorry, Cledo,' he told the dog. 'You were very brave, but I shouldn't have sent you against a creature like that one.'

The dog raised his head and looked at Pettic as if to say, 'I'd like see you stop me!'

Klondor returned with the herbs and a waterskin of water. He poured some of the water onto Cledo's wounds and gently wiped them. Then he covered them with the herbs and bound a cloth around the dog's middle to hold them in place.

'We should stay here in the cave to let the herbs begin to do their job,' he told Pettic. 'Can you lift Cledo and take him inside?'

Between them they got the large dog into the cave. It smelled of boar but they decided they could put up with it. Once Pettic was satisfied Cledo was comfortable the pair went out to butcher the boar. Its skin would be worth quite a lot, Klondor said, as they skinned the creature before butchering the carcass. They took some of the offal into the cave and gave it to a grateful Cledo along with a bowl of water Then Klondor lit a fire to cook some of the boar meat, which they ate with gusto.

That evening Pettic told Klondor of his worry the boar had fathered some piglets. They decided they had better search the area for any herds of sows to see if any had white piglets, or any that seemed extra large. They would have to wipe them out if they wanted to rid the area of this menace forever.

The next morning, leaving Cledo in the cave with strict instructions to stay where he was, the pair set off to scour the surroundings. They had no success during the morning, but in the afternoon spotted signs of a herd of sows with piglets. They tracked them to a clearing in the wood.

Sure enough, there was the herd. Most of the piglets were normal, with dark stripes running down their backs but there were two pure white ones and one that looked rather large, although it was difficult to say if it were exceptional or not.

Pettic decided it was not worth the risk and so he nocked an arrow and let fly at one of the white ones while Klondor threw a javelin at the large one. This spooked the herd and they began to run.

There was still one white piglet alive. They needed to kill it too. Noting the direction the herd had gone they went to collect the two dead piglets.

'A pity to kill these,' sighed Pettic. 'Only babies, too. They had no chance of a life, poor little things.'

After carrying the dead piglets back to the cave and checking on Cledo, they went after the herd again. This time they managed to kill the remaining white piglet with no trouble and took it back to the others. As the sun crept lower and lower in the sky they settled down for the night.

Cledo seemed a little better the next morning. Klondor put some herbs in his water but the dog refused to drink it. All the persuasion Pettic used failed to get him to drink the herbs. He took some liver from one of the piglets, chopped it up and mixed it with some of the herbs. The dog gobbled it down not noticing the unusual taste, or if he did, it was not strong enough to trouble him.

The two young men decided to stay in the cave until Cledo was well enough to walk a reasonable distance. Klondor worried about infection, because the wild pigs were known to carry a number of diseases, but as the next couple of days passed and the dog showed no sign of sickness, Klondor began to be hopeful that he would recover fully.

It took a week before Cledo could walk well enough for them to leave. They loaded the meat and skins into their packs. The temperature in the cave had been cool enough so it had not spoiled.

They approached the lake and the village on its banks. A couple of women, who were down at the water's edge, spotted them. The two ran back to their village and by the time the pair reached it, a deputation of men approached demanding to know if they had been successful in their hunt.

It surprised Pettic that this neighbouring village knew of their hunt, but then news was always readily learned.

Klondor pulled the boar skin from his pack and spread it on the ground.

'It wasn't a phantom at all, you see,' he told the assembled people, 'just a regular animal. It was large, yes, but it was what Pettic called an albino. That is an animal born with no pigment in its skin. Albinos have red eyes too, which added to its frightening appearance.'

'Why did it only come out at night?' asked someone in the gathering.

Pettic answered. 'Because it had no pigment the sun burned it very easily. You people live in a place with strong sunlight and so you have dark skin. The dark pigment helps to protect you from burning. I come from a cooler land and so I don't need so much pigment. This animal had none of the protective pigment and it needed to keep away from the sun. It spent the days in a cave.'

The headman of the Lake Village insisted they come in to celebrate the end of the boar. Klondor told Pettic they must accept or it would be a slight on the village, and so they followed the villagers. To his surprise, as they entered the square, his earring began to feel warm

The headman took them to his own hut while the people prepared a feast. Pettic glanced round, but in the dim light he could see little. He knew the emerald was here in this village somewhere. Still, he could do nothing about it in the present circumstances so he settled down to talk to the headman about how they managed to kill the boar, and to tell him about how they had also killed the piglets he had fathered.

As darkness fell, The impromptu feast began. They had been told which of the huts had been prepared for them to sleep in after the feast, and they put their things in it. After that they went down to the lake to bathe. They had not been able to wash properly in the pool by the boar's cave as it had been very muddy, churned up by the animal's feet. When they felt clean they went to attend the feast.

They were guests of honour and sat on either side of the headman, who told them his name was Shillor. His children, two young boys of about thirteen and eleven and two daughters, one of whom was about sixteen and the other about ten, sat on each side of Pettic and Klondor. Cledo was also included in the feast. He lay at Pettic's feet and Pettic gave him choice bits of meat. The two young boys especially fussed the dog, and he lapped up the attention.

Pettic decided he would not drink the amount he had at the feast prior to their leaving Klondor's village. They both thought they should leave early the next morning. They had already been gone longer than they thought, what with Cledo's injury and hunting the piglets.

Besides, they wanted to get back before the meat spoiled. Klondor had packed it with preserving herbs and spices, but that did not guarantee it would not spoil if kept out in the heat too long. They ate and drank sparingly, in spite of being encouraged by everyone to indulge themselves.

Halfway through the meal, the chief priest of the village stood up.

'We must thank Holy Jakim for his help in ridding us of this menace. Perhaps it was sent to torment us as some kind of punishment. Perhaps we had not respected the animals that Holy Jakim has sent to us for our food, or perhaps we had not thanked Holy Jakim well enough for his help in the hunt. Whatever the cause, let us now thank him for sending his servants, Pettic and his hound, Cledo, from another world to help us destroy this beast that has so harmed us.

'Holy Jakim, accept our thanks and our offerings to you. We apologise to the White Boar that we had to kill him, and also to his children, the three piglets, that also had to be killed to prevent further dangers in future. We are truly sorry that they could not have the life they should have had. This we regret, but it was necessary for our safety.'

The assembled villagers all responded with 'Sorry, Holy Jakim. Sorry, White Boar. Sorry, piglets,' then resumed their meal.

Chapter 6

The next day Pettic and Klondor left Lake Village and continued to their own. They arrived just as the villagers were leaving the fields to return to their homes. Borrin spotted them and with a roar, ran towards them where he embraced Klondor saying, 'My son, my son, you're alive,' over and over again. Then he turned to Pettic and embraced him.

'Thank you for bringing my son back alive. It's been so long I was sure you'd both been killed. What of your quest? Did you succeed? No, don't tell me yet. You can tell your story before the whole village tomorrow. I'm sure you want nothing more than rest tonight.'

'First, father, I think you should know we've killed the 'phantom' boar. It was as Pettic said—not a phantom at all but what he called an albino. We also tracked down three piglets that he had fathered and looked as if they may have inherited some of his characteristics. We've the meat from him and from the piglets as well as his skin.'

After eating, the friends went to their huts to sleep.

The following morning no one went to the fields. Everyone wanted to hear about the hunt for the phantom boar. Pettic decided Klondor should tell the tale and so the young man stood up before the assembled villagers and regaled them with the tale of the boar hunt. If he exaggerated a bit in places, who could blame him?

He gave Cledo his due honours saying the brave dog nearly lost his life trying to save him. That the wolfhound only received a cut, albeit a long and deep one, he did not mention. Pettic, he told the awed people, saved his life when he tripped over a tree root. He could not praise his friend highly enough. Pettic felt embarrassed at this flattery and bowed his head to hide his blushes.

After the tale was told, people called out questions and the pair answered as truthfully as possible, trying to remember what Klondor had said so as not to contradict his tale. If there were a few discrepancies the people let them pass.

That day the villagers did no work and there was much rejoicing. People drank too much, the chief priest prayed too much, the children made too much noise, Borrin and his wife laughed too much, the village dogs barked too much, and everyone ate too much.

Klondor and Pettic took the boar meat out of the packs and some of the women cooked it in fire pits. Other pieces they hung over the fire to smoke. They treated the three piglets in the same way. There would be meat for quite some time in the village.

A tanner took the boar's skin away to be cured. The pure white skin would be very valuable. Klondor told Pettic that he ought to have the skin as a reward for his part in the killing.

At the end of the day Pettic retired to his hut feeling pleased his part in the hunt had been so well received, but still anxious to get on with getting the emerald, both to help to find Torren and to get him back to his world.

The following morning, Borrin summoned him.

'I can't tell you how grateful my wife and I are that you've killed the boar and brought our son back safely. She was most anxious until you arrived, being certain he had been killed.

We're now safe from this menace. Why do you think he started to kill people?'

'Well,' began Pettic, 'I can't be sure, really. It may be, being such a large animal, he could not satisfy his appetite by anything he found in the forest. He couldn't have caught the deer, I don't think, so maybe he found people an easy prey.' Pettic shrugged then continued.

'Boars aren't usually hunters, but they'll take what they can find. Of course, it could be a revenge attack. He may have decided people were a danger to him so he attacked when he saw them rather than skulk in the undergrowth. Pigs are intelligent animals, you know.'

Borrin looked thoughtful and then said, 'Still, he's gone now, so we must talk of your reward. If I had that emerald of which you talk I would readily give it to you, but I have nothing of such value except one thing only. My daughter, Rolinda. If you wish to take her as your wife, I'll gratefully give her to you.'

Pettic looked at the headman in astonishment.

'Your daughter is a truly beautiful girl,' he replied, 'and I am honoured you would think me worthy of her, but I cannot stay here on Terra. I must find this emerald and return to my own world. I couldn't take her with me, as it would not be fair of me to expect her to come away from her family and friends. She'd be going to an entirely different life. One she can't imagine. I'm grateful for your offer, but I'm afraid I can't accept it.'

'I thought you'd say that. You must take the boar skin then. You must have a reward for your help in this.'

Pettic told the headman if he would help him to acquire the emerald, that would be the only reward he needed.

The headman then began to talk of ways the sword could be stolen. At this point, Klondor came out of the hut. On hearing this, he remonstrated with his father.

'You can't do this,' he said. 'If anyone found out we had any-thing to do with the theft it would mean war between our villages.'

'There've been wars before, son, and there'll be wars again. Don't tell me you're afraid of war. I had you down for a warrior, not a milksop.'

'Oh, father, I'm not afraid of war. It's just that I don't want a war with the Lake Village. There's this girl there…'

His father interrupted him. 'I should have guessed there was a girl involved. What is it you want?'

'I came out to ask your permission to court her. She's the headman's daughter and I met her at the feast they threw for us when we stopped there on our way back from killing the boar.'

Klondor smiled and said, 'Father, she's the most beautiful thing I've ever seen. Her hair is a wonderful blue-black and shines in the sunshine like, like…Oh, I can't think of anything that shines so beautifully. Her eyes are like pieces of jet and her skin is soft as a baby's. She speaks gently, like the soft showers of the springtime and when she smiles, all my troubles disappear.'

Pettic looked at his friend in amazement, and Borrin said, 'She seems to have turned you into a poet, lad. Still, if you've set your heart on courting her, then you have my permission. You must go to the Lake Village, of course and get her mother's permission too.' He turned to Pettic. 'He'll need someone to speak for him to her mother. Will you go and do this task? It will give you a chance to try to seek out this gem you want so badly.'

Pettic looked at Klondor and back at the young man's father. 'I have two questions,' he said. 'Firstly, why does Klondor need to speak to her mother and not her father, and secondly, I have no idea what the form is. What should I say?

'A young man must speak to his father and a young woman her mother. If the young man is asking permission to begin a courtship, then he asks the girl's mother, and if a young girl is asking to begin a courtship with a young man, then she must ask his father. As to what you must say, Klondor will no doubt tell you plenty of things in his favour as you will have to 'sell' him to the girl's mother. He'll also tell you the correct forms to use.'

Pettic readily agreed both to help his friend and to try to find the sword with the gem. The pair made their way to Pettic's hut for Klondor to brief him about what he was to say. They agreed they should not rush back to Lake Village. It did not do to seem too eager, but for the next few days, Klondor was in a state of nerves.

'What if someone else offers for her?' he asked on the third day. 'She's so beautiful I'm sure there must be someone else who wants her. Someone from the Forest Village, maybe. Perhaps he's there now asking permission to court her. What if she prefers him to me? Maybe there's a young man in her village who's already asked to court her. Maybe the man from the Forest Village has already asked.'

He went on like this for some time, convincing himself she had already got a suitor, until Pettic got thoroughly tired of it and told him, laughingly, if he did not stop worrying about something that may never happen he would withdraw from being his sponsor. This stopped Klondor in his tracks and he said no more. But by his expression he had not stopped worrying.

Eventually the day came when they were to go to visit. They set off early in the morning. Klondor's mother gave them both strict instructions to make sure they arrived at the Lake Village in the same state they left their own; that is, with pristine white robes and hair neatly combed.

'I don't want my future daughter-in-law to think we are a dirty, scruffy tribe,' she told them.

Klondor laughed. 'If she thinks that then she won't become your daughter-in-law, now, will she. She'll dismiss me and take on one of the other suitors from the Forest Village or from her own village.'

Pettic punched his friend. 'Those suitors are all in your imagination. You've no evidence they exist at all.'

With that, the pair, along with Cledo, set off towards the lake.

It was an hour before nightfall when they finally arrived at Lake Village. They stood outside the palisade and called out to ask admittance. Soon someone came running out.

'Come in,' he said. 'We are pleased to see you. The headman will also be pleased to welcome the Phantom Boar Killers.'

He ran back through the gate to tell everyone of their arrival. Soon they were surrounded by villagers and could hardly make their way through the press. Eventually they reached the headman's hut and stood to one side waiting. The headman was hearing both sides of a dispute between the villagers and had to pronounce his verdict before he could talk to the two.

When the dispute had been resolved to the satisfaction of all, the headman turned to Pettic and Klondor.

'We're delighted to see you both here again so soon,' he boomed. Everything about this man was large. 'You'll eat with my family this evening. I'm sure you're here for a reason, but we'll leave business until daylight tomorrow. Much better to do business in the daylight, I find.'

Poor Klondor had another night to wait. He again sat next to the headman's elder daughter. This time he discovered she was called Beline. He whispered to her that he thought it a pretty name and she giggled. Her mother glanced at her severely though and she stopped.

Klondor barely slept a wink that night. Neither did Pettic. Klondor asked him almost every half hour if he thought Beline liked him. On receiving the reply that he, Pettic, was sure she did, he went on to ask, 'But does she like me *enough*? Does she like me *in that way*?'

Pettic sighed and resigned himself to a sleepless night.

Early the next morning, after they had broken the night's fast, the pair went to wait before the steps of the headman's hut. It seemed an age to Klondor, but eventually the headman came out.

'Now, what is it you two want. I think it's a boon because of the way you're dressed, in your best white robes. Speak up then,' he added after both young men looked nervously at each other.

Klondor knelt down on the ground and Pettic began his speech.

'Sir,' he began, 'my friend kneels before you in supplication. He knows he is not worthy, but he wished to ask one thing and one thing only. That thing is that he be allowed to pay court to your eldest daughter, the beautiful Beline.'

Here the headman stopped him. 'My wife is the one you should be putting this request to, not me. I'll go and get her.'

He entered the hut and shortly came out with his wife, as tiny a woman as her husband was large, but with a fierce, independent look in her eye. She spoke to Pettic.

'I understand you have a petition to present to me,' she said, turning to look at both young men in turn.

'Yes, madam,' Pettic told her. 'My friend wishes to court your most beautiful daughter, Beline. He has admired her since meeting her when we stayed here after killing the boar. He has hardly slept for thinking of her. He has hardly eaten for fear that she would have committed to another. He has bored all his friends near to death with his tales of her beauty. In truth, he had turned from warrior into poet.

'I can vouch for my friend in every way. He is brave and loyal. I would not wish to have another beside me in a fight. He fought bravely against the boar and put his life at risk when he thought I might lose mine. He is honest and true.

'In the time I have known him he has not told an untruth. He is kind and generous, always putting others before himself. His health is excellent and he is strong as an ox. He will father strong babies, and plenty of them. All in all, he is as close to a perfect specimen of manhood you could with to meet.'

'I am glad he's so perfect,' replied the little woman with a twinkle in her eye. 'It's rare to meet someone quite without flaws. What does Beline think of this?' She turned to Klondor as she asked this.

He looked up at her and said, 'Beline? I...I don't know. I haven't asked her. I thought I should speak to you first.'

'Most unusual,' replied the girl's mother. 'Usually the young folk have done some courting before arriving at this stage. Some have done quite a lot, in fact. So much that a wedding is inevitable. I think we should ask Beline what she thinks of all this.'

Klondor sighed. This was not going at all how he had imagined it. Was Beline going to accept his suit or was she going to reject him because he had not spoken about it to her before speaking to her parents?

Just then Beline herself came out of the hut, and Klondor could see the shadows of the smaller children lurking in the dimness.

The headman spoke to his daughter.

'Beline, my sweet,' he said. 'Here we have a young man asking permission to court you, but he says he's said nothing to you. What do you think of that?'

Beline smiled at Klondor and then replied to her father, without taking her eyes from Klondor's.

'Father,' she said, 'I think that here we have a young man who's anxious to do the right thing. That is good, I think. So many young men don't obey the customs and rules of our society and seek to court young women secretly without asking their parents.' She then turned to her father and grinned. 'Besides, he's such a handsome young man.'

Her mother then turned to Pettic and some of the formality returned.

'You have spoken eloquently, Pettic, in praise of your friend. I cannot believe he is as perfect as you suggest,' Klondor looked down at the ground and sighed. *Here it comes. She's going to reject my suit.'*

The headman's wife continued. 'However, my daughter has a good point in that he has done the correct thing and come to us first. My daughter also seems to look favourably on the young man and so I say that if he wishes, he can court her.'

The sigh that escaped Klondor could be heard all over the village square until the clapping started. Klondor stood up and went over to Beline and kissed her on the cheek. The couple then held hands and stood in front of the assembled village to receive the cheers.

This was not usual for just permission granted for a courtship, but so high was Klondor in their estimation they were delighted he was courting one of their own girls. Here was a real life hero who was going to be associated, if only by marriage, to them.

Klondor and Pettic stayed in Lake Village for a week so the young people could get to know each other. After all, they had only met very briefly over a meal. Klondor spent every waking moment with Beline. This gave Pettic a good chance to wander around searching for a likely place for the sword to be stored.

The first place he approached was the armoury hut but his earring did not get appreciably warmer. In fact, he thought it was a little cooler than it had been when he was in the centre of the village. He went back there and stood looking round.

It was difficult for him because he was no less a hero to these people than Klondor, and with his light skin, hair and eyes he seemed exotic. A group of people always surrounded him when they were not actually working and the girls would hardly leave him alone.

At first he enjoyed this attention, but as the week wore on he became more frustrated. He smiled at the people and answered their questions as politely as he could. They wanted to know all about his home world and how he had come here.

'Do people speak the same language in your world as we do here?' asked one young man.

'No,' replied Pettic. 'I can understand you, and you me only by magic.'

There was an indrawing of breath when he said this and lots of questions. He gave the same demonstration he had given in Hill Village, removing his amulet and talking. They were amazed there was a world with magic.

Pettic did not tell them of his true reason for coming to this world, or that he needed the emerald to return. They asked him how long he intended to stay on Terra, and he made vague sounds. When asked how he was going to get back, he simply said 'The same way I came—with magic.' That was true enough. It was by magic. Just not any magic he had with him at the moment.

Soon he was able to leave the gathering and continue his search. It reminded him of a game he had played as a child where someone hid an object and he had to find it, getting clues such as 'You're getting warmer, no colder. You're freezing or you're so hot you're nearly on fire.' He smiled to himself at the memory and thought that this time the hot and cold analogy was true. He continued his search.

As he approached the headman's hut his earring got really warm. It became almost uncomfortable. The nearer he approached the hut the warmer it seemed to be. By walking round the hut he decided the emerald was inside near the back.

This was a problem. How could he get it without anyone seeing him, or suspecting him? It would either ruin Klondor's courtship, cause war between the two villages or both if he were caught, or even suspected. Therefore he left to ponder the problem.

Every evening Klondor returned to the hut they were sharing and regaled Pettic with tales of Beline's beauty, her kindness, her gentle manner and every other virtue he could think of. She was just perfect in his eyes. He resolved he was going to marry her and at the end of the week, he asked her if she would have him.

Beline's eyes lit up and she accepted. Then he had to go to her mother for her permission, which she readily granted, before he and Pettic left to return to Hill Village to ask permission of his father.

Chapter 7

Once back in Hill Village, Klondor lost no time in going to his father. Fortunately the villagers had finished their work for the day and so Borrin was just washing himself in preparation for the evening meal. When he saw Klondor and Pettic he stopped and stood waiting for them to approach.

'Well,' he asked, 'How did it go? We assume her mother gave permission for you to court her or you'd have been back before now.'

'Father, it was perfect. She's perfect. Her mother was pleased to allow me to court her.'

His mother then came out of the hut and saw Klondor.

'Well, at least tell us her name,' she said.

'Sorry mother. She's called Beline. Mother, she's even more perfect than I thought.' He started on a description of Beline's charms.

'I have no doubt you think she's perfect, son, but just remember there is no such thing as perfection.'

'Yes, mother, but she's as near as a human being can be. I won't find anyone else who can compare.' He turned to his father. 'I want your permission for a betrothal father,' he said.

His father smiled. This he had been expecting. 'I'd like to have met her before the betrothal, but if she's your choice, then I give you my permission.' he said.

The smile on Klondor's face nearly split it in half. Pettic thought his muscles would surely tear if he strained them any more. He thanked his father profusely. Pettic thought anyone watching would have thought the headman had given his son a fortune in riches. On reflection, Pettic thought, perhaps he had.

Klondor's mother then turned to practicalities and decided it was time to eat. She asked Pettic to eat with them and he gratefully accepted. During the meal Klondor regaled everyone again with the charms of his soon to be betrothed. His siblings were interested as they had not heard the discussions going on outside, especially Rolinda. She was now of marriageable age and was looking at every young man as a possible husband.

'What are you going to give her as a betrothal gift?' she asked Klondor. 'It must be something of great value or she'll think you don't value her enough. She could even break off the betrothal before it has begun!'

Klondor looked in panic around his family.

'I don't have anything of great value,' he said. 'What can I give her?'

'We'll think of something, son,' his father said. 'Don't you worry. Your sister's worrying you unnecessarily.'

Later, Pettic lay in bed thinking how he could help his friend and eventually came up with an idea.

The next morning, with Klondor still feeling depressed at not having a valuable gift for Beline, Pettic told him what he thought.

'You know the boar hide you gave me, Klondor?' he began.

'What of it?' replied his friend.

'It should be nearly cured now and you yourself said how valuable it is. Suppose I give it to you for Beline?'

'You'd do that for me? It's very generous, but I can't accept. It's yours.'

'We both had a hand in killing that animal, Klondor. You have as much right to it as I have, you know.'

'But it was you who made the killing blow, Pettic. I was helpless on the ground.'

'Doesn't matter. If there had been only me and not three of us to give it pause it wouldn't be the boar that's dead, but me. No, we all three had a hand in the kill. I willingly give it to you.'

Klondor thought for a moment then he accepted with a laugh and clapped his friend on the back.

'Never has a man had a better friend. I thank you with all my heart. I half hope you can't find that blasted gem to take you back to your own world, then you'll have to stay here and I won't lose my best friend.'

'Pettic smiled back at Klondor. 'I, too, will be sorry to part, but I must go. It's my duty to my king and to my country to do so. However, if I can't get the gem, then I'll not be too unhappy here.'

He sighed and thought for a moment about Lucenra and Torren and how he would miss both of them. They had also been his very good friends. He would miss them both if he could not get back to his world. Still, he would have to wait and see what happened.

After a week in Hill Village, Klondor was anxious to return to Lake Village to ask for a betrothal with Beline. He told Pettic he missed her more than he thought he could miss anyone, so they arranged to return the following day.

The skin was now cured and Klondor packed it up carefully so it would not have any creases or marks on it when he presented it to her. His parents said they wanted to meet this paragon and so would follow on with the rest of their children in a couple of days' time.

Klondor seemed jittery for the rest of the day, being unable to sit still for very long, or concentrate on the work in the fields. Pettic was pleased when night fell and he retired to his hut. Being with Klondor in such a state was very wearing. He lay down on his bed with Cledo and talked to the dog.

'Klondor's getting a bit obsessive about this girl, I think,' he told Cledo. 'Is this how love takes people? I hope I don't get in such a state over a girl, though I can't see me doing so.'

In reply the wolfhound licked his face and lay down as if to say *go to sleep and stop worrying.*

Klondor arrived before dawn the next morning. Pettic was not awake. Cledo barked once and rushed out of the sleeping room to greet his master's friend. Pettic rose reluctantly and wandered out to see that his friend had arrived with breakfast prepared.

'Come on, lazy bones,' laughed Klondor. 'We need to set off early.'

'Why?' yawned Pettic, still half-asleep. 'What's happening today besides work?'

Klondor punched him and laughed.

'You know full well what's happening, Pettic,' he said. 'Get dressed. I want to go as soon as possible to get back to my Beline.'

'She's not yours yet, friend,' Pettic said. 'She may turn you down.'

Nothing seemed to shake Klondor's mood, however, and soon the pair, along with Cledo once more set off along the path to Lake Village.

On the way, Klondor asked Pettic if he had not seen a girl that he would like to court. He wanted all the world to share the same happiness he had. When Pettic answered in the negative, Klondor said he hoped it would not be too long before he did so.

They arrived at Lake Village in the late afternoon. Since they left before the sun rose they arrived well before it set. They waited outside the palisade and called for someone to answer and let them in. It was not considered polite to just enter the village without permission.

Soon a young man opened the gates and said, 'Enter, heroes of the Phantom Boar, and be welcome.'

As soon as they passed the gates, Beline came rushing over and embraced Klondor in an unseemly manner. At least that is what her mother told her later. Klondor, however, was delighted to receive such an exuberant welcome and all his fears of a change of heart on the part of Beline were set to rest.

The young man approached her parents.

'My family wishes to meet with your daughter,' he told them. 'They will be coming along in a few days' time. They have received many good words about her from me. I don't think they believe me as to how perfect she is and want to see for themselves.'

Beline's father smiled. He remembered being in love that way and looked at his tiny wife and a knowing look passed between them. She looked up at him and smiled back.

'They will be most welcome here,' she said. 'Of course, we do know one another, being head families of our respective villages, but we don't know one another's families. It's only natural they'll want to meet our daughter in case anything comes of this courtship.'

Here she looked enquiringly at Klondor, but he gave nothing away.

'You must eat and then sleep. You're sure to be tired after your long walk,' the headman told them. 'We'll talk tomorrow. I suppose you know your way to the guest hut?'

During the evening, Klondor managed to catch a few minutes alone with Beline. He asked her what she felt about them becoming betrothed. The girl was all enthusiasm and begged Klondor to ask her mother as soon as possible. This he did the next morning and upon receiving her agreement rushed to tell Pettic.

Pettic clapped Klondor on the back and grinned in pleasure as he saw his friend's happiness.

Beline's parents decided to hold the formal betrothal ceremony as soon as Klondor's family arrived, and Klondor spent as much of that time as he could with Beline.

To Pettic, the couple of days until Klondor's family arrived went very quickly, but to Klondor, waiting for the betrothal ceremony, they dragged, but soon the day arrived.

Rolinda expressed delight in Klondor's chosen bride and the pair were soon friends. Klondor was pleased with this, as he had been secretly afraid they would not get on. His parents expressed their views that his chosen bride was almost as perfect as he had described and so Klondor's joy knew no bounds. The only thing that marred his happiness was that he did not see how he could get the sword for his friend.

Two days after the arrival of Klondor's family they held the betrothal ceremony. Both young people dressed in their best. Klondor's mother had brought a new white robe for him to wear, trimmed with red at the base.

Beline wore a blue robe with white embroidery round the bottom. She wore white flowers in her hair and Klondor thought she looked more beautiful than ever. Pettic thought so too and grinned at Klondor's face as he looked at Beline.

Everyone was in attendance at the event, even Cledo, who was considered an honorary human being for the day. After all, he had helped on the Phantom Boar Hunt. He enjoyed every minute of it.

The Chief Priest stood up and intoned a prayer to Tremm, the god of marriage and the family, entreating him to bless the young couple who were promising to wed, then he heard them say their oaths of betrothal. After that came the giving of the betrothal gifts.

'I hereby present you with this gift as a token of my esteem,' said Klondor, following the traditional wording. He took the boar skin from his pack that Pettic brought over and spread it out before her. A gasp went up from the crowd. It was perfect and had kept its white colour through the tanning process. The tanners of Hill Village had taken great care not to spoil it with any stains. Beline accepted the gift with grace and then presented her own.

'I hereby present you with this gift as a token of my esteem.'

Her father went into his hut and, after a few minutes, longer than anyone had thought it would take to pick up the gift, he brought a parcel over and Beline undid it and presented it to Klondor. Pettic's earring felt as if it were burning a hole in his ear, for in the wrapping was nothing less than a sword with an emerald gleaming in its hilt.

There was an intake of breath from the assembled people at this most generous gift. They all knew how their headman had treasured this sword since finding it in a cave to the north of the village.

'This is too much,' Klondor gasped in amazement. 'It is far more valuable than my gift.'

The headman stepped forward and stood in front of Klondor.

'Son,' he said, 'This was not the original gift Beline was going to give you, but when I saw what you gave her I decided it was more appropriate. The gift you gave her was fought for in blood. In getting that skin, you saved many lives at the risk of your own. No, your gift is of far greater worth than this sword.'

Klondor could scarcely believe his eyes. Here was the sword Pettic had been trying to think of a way to get without bloodshed, and he had received it into his hands freely. He could hardly believe his luck. Now Pettic could leave Terra and go back to his world. He was both happy and sad. Happy for his friend and for his betrothal, but sad he would lose his friend.

The feasting went on for two days. Pettic wondered what the feasting would be like for a wedding if it were like this for a betrothal. He also wondered if Klondor would, or could give him the sword.

He worried about this. He thought Klondor would want to give him the sword, but would it put his betrothal at risk? Would he be willing to risk it? Pettic continued to worry all through the feast but no one seemed to notice except for Cledo, who laid his head on his master's knee and looked up at him with soulful eyes.

Two days later, after the end of the betrothal ceremony and party, the two sets of parents met to discuss when the wedding would take place. Since the time between the courtship and betrothal had been unprecedently short, they thought there should be a longer time before the wedding. They agreed on a year, much to the disappointment of the young couple who hoped they would agree to a shorter time. Soon afterwards, the family from the Hill Village along with Pettic, left to return home.

When they arrived it was evening and everyone went straight to their beds. The next day, just before work started, Klondor arrived at Pettic's hut.

'I've been awake all night, Pettic,' he began. 'I've a terrible decision to make. Here in my possession is the thing you need both to return to your world and to help to release your Crown Prince. However, this object was the betrothal gift of my Beline. What will this do to our betrothal if I give her gift to you? I know I would be upset if she gave away my gift to her.'

Pettic felt unable to respond to this comment. He, too, was torn, because he did not want to harm Klondor's betrothal, but he desperately wanted to get back to his own world and rescue Torren. Eventually he said, 'Why don't you ask Beline what she thinks? It's only a day to Lake Village after all.'

They agreed that the next day Klondor would travel to see Beline and ask her what she thought.

He set off early. He was not reluctant to go, of course, and this time he was going alone. Pettic thought it would be better if he were not there, as his presence might cause embarrassment.

Pettic decided he would help out with the stock while Klondor was away. His parents had a couple of cows and some sheep so he had worked with animals from an early age. The stock in the village was mainly pigs and goats, but milking a goat was not much different from milking a cow, except lower down, and the other tasks were similar.

He was enjoying himself in spite of his anxiety to get back to his home. He wondered how his parents were getting on. When he had been made an earl, he had been given the lands and castle of the dead earl and had moved his parents and brother into it. They sold their farm and were now running his much larger establishment. Pettic hoped they could cope with this extra workload and he wondered how his mother was handling running a household of servants. She had never had a servant in her life before this.

Klondor arrived at Lake Village and found the usual welcome. Beline was working in the fields when he got there. As it was getting near to sunset, he did not have long to wait before she came back to the village. She saw him as soon as she passed through the gate, but in truth, she could hardly have missed him.

Klondor had positioned himself immediately through the gate and was leaning nonchalantly against the palisade. When she saw him, she gave a little squeal of delight and rushed over to embrace him. The other people coming home smiled to see this demonstration of affection, not a few of them remembering themselves in the first stages of love.

'I didn't expect to see you for a few weeks, Klondor,' she exclaimed. 'I'm so pleased you're here, but why are you back so soon?'

'I've something to discuss with you, my love,' responded her betrothed. 'However, it will wait until tomorrow. I want to enjoy just being with you tonight.'

Beline's curiosity had to wait. The couple spent the next few hours in talk and kisses.

Next morning, Beline's father excused work for her. She took Klondor into the family hut.

'See, Klondor,' she said. 'I have your betrothal gift on my bed so I can think of you as I go to sleep and hope to dream of you.'

Klondor was a bit embarrassed about this since he was about to ask her if he could give her gift away. There was no way he could do so without her knowing, so he had to ask. This was going to be the hardest thing he had ever done. How would she take it? Would she think it showed a lack of care on his part? He took a deep breath and plunged ahead as the only thing he could do.

'It's about your betrothal gift. I need to speak to you about it,' he began.

'Is it not good enough? Don't you like it?'

'It's a wonderful gift. So valuable. I know how your father valued it as well. This is very hard for me, my love. I think I'd better tell you the whole story. This is about Pettic and why he came to this world of Terra.'

Klondor went on to tell Beline about the impersonation of the Crown Prince of Ponderia and his abduction. He told her Pettic had followed the impersonator and seen he was, in truth, not Torren. He spoke of the visit to the court magician and how he told Pettic about the other worlds and how to get there. He then told her about the gems that were needed both to release the true prince and to allow Pettic to return to his own world.'

'So you're here to ask if you can give my betrothal gift to your friend,' observed Beline.

Klondor hung his head as he replied. 'Yes,' he muttered.

Beline put her head on one side and examined her lover.

'I'll need to think about this and maybe ask advice. I'll take the rest of today and tell you tomorrow.'

As she stood up and escorted Klondor out of her parents' hut he turned to her and said, 'This doesn't mean I don't care about you or that I don't value your gift, but perhaps the future of an entire country depends on this. Pettic tells me this impostor is cruel and self-indulgent.'

'I'll see you about it tomorrow, Klondor. You'd better go and leave me now.'

Klondor returned to his hut where he spent the long day lying on his bed worrying that he might have put his betrothal at risk in his desire to help his friend.

After a sleepless night, dawn eventually came and Klondor left his hut. People were preparing to go to work. They waved or hailed Klondor as he passed. Klondor half-heartedly responded and the villagers wondered what argument between the young couple had caused this.

Eventually, Beline came out from the hut with her family. They left for their work, leaving Beline to talk to Klondor. She approached him quietly and beckoned him onto the veranda.

The pair sat down on the mats and Beline began.

'This was very difficult, Klondor. As you must know, to give away a betrothal gift is the biggest insult you can give to a girl. I began to doubt you loved me enough for a marriage.'

At this comment, Klondor hung his head. He began to protest, but Beline stopped him.

'Let me finish, please, Klondor. On further reflection I decided you did care and that's why you're asking me. If you really didn't care enough to worry about insulting me you would have simply given the sword to Pettic and hoped I wouldn't find out. No, I think this shows what a caring young man you are. You're obviously torn. You want to help your friend and not insult me either. It can't have been easy for you to come to ask me this. That was very brave too. You also care about someone you have never met, simply because your friend cares for him. You're a wonderful human being, my darling, and so I give you permission to give the sword to Pettic.'

Then she kissed him and stood up. 'You'd better go and tell Pettic he can go home, hadn't you? I'll come to your village in a couple of weeks.'

With that she left a startled Klondor looking after her.

Chapter 8

The three days since Klondor left seemed like three years to Pettic. He was particularly anxious because of what Blundo told him about the time passing differently in the other worlds. He did not know if minutes or years had passed in his world while he was in the world of Terra. This made him all the more anxious to get back.

He would be sorry to leave the friends he had made here, but he did miss his home world. This was a much more primitive place with the huts being built of mud and thatch, not stone. Everything they had was either grown by themselves, made from the materials they found or from the animals they hunted. True, they wasted very little, but Pettic did miss some of the comforts of home.

By the evening of the third day, anyone looking for him would find Pettic standing at the gate leading to Lake Village. As the sun sank below the hills behind him, he saw a figure on the road. He ran to meet it. The friends embraced and walked up to the village in companionable silence. Pettic did not want to seem to be too anxious to leave Terra so he curbed his impatience.

When they arrived through the village gates, Klondor led Pettic to the guest hut where he was staying.

'I spoke to Beline,' he began. 'She gave me a lecture on how important the betrothal gifts are and what an insult it is to part with them. I was very downhearted at this, but then she told me she'd think about it and let me know the next day what she'd decided. I hardly slept at all last night, Pettic. I was so worried she would refuse and also that she would be so insulted she'd break off the betrothal.'

Here he paused and Pettic held his breath.

'This morning she came to me and talked again at length. She talked about my bravery and what a good friend I am to be seeking to give away what must be very close to my heart (which indeed it is, as I reassured her). She then talked about nobility and honour. But to get to the point, she's agreed I can give the sword to you.'

Pettic embraced his friend. 'I thank you with all my heart. You've risked losing the girl you love for me and my country. A country you don't know, and will never know. I can't do anything for you in return.'

Klondor smiled. 'You killed the boar, remember. That has saved many lives and, incidentally, its skin has helped me win the love of Beline. No, you don't need to do any more for me or any of us here on Terra. When will you leave?'

'I'd like to go as soon as possible. I need to say my goodbyes to your family and some others here in Hill Village. I want to go soon because I don't know how long has passed on my world. It could be days, weeks or years, but I hope it's not years! Will you say my goodbyes to Beline for me. She's a beautiful girl with a beautiful nature to match. I'm sure you'll both be very happy.'

The two young men who had found such friendship in a short time embraced each other, and if there were tears in their eyes, well, who could blame them.

The goodbyes took longer than Pettic had thought. Everyone in the village wanted to shake his hand. He was, after all, the man who had rescued them from the 'Phantom Boar'. They found him an interesting visitor too, having come from a different world and one that had magic too. That he knew little about the art himself made no difference. He had a magic amulet to let him speak to them and understand their language. What was more, he was searching for a sword that had a gem imbued with magic.

The people would have scoffed at the thought of magic not long ago, but now everyone acknowledged its existence, if not on their world.

Cledo also came in for much fussing, especially from the children with whom he had played and obviously loved. He had been with children ever since he first came to the royal nursery as a pup and enjoyed their company still.

Eventually, after half the day had gone, the villagers let Pettic go. He collected his few things and went to say his farewells to Borrin and his family. Klondor told him they were all going to come up to the cave to see him off, and, truth to tell, they all wanted to see for themselves how he was going to walk through a wall. Woller was to be in attendance too.

The party ascended the path, down which Pettic had come with the priests, to the Holy Cave. They entered the large cavern with the square stone altar in the centre. The passage led off from the right hand side at the back. The party entered it. It was a tight squeeze as it was not very large, but somehow everyone managed to get in. Rolinda cried as Pettic embraced each of the family in turn and then, gripping Cledo firmly by the scruff of his neck, and hoping the dog would come through with him, he strode towards the cave wall.

Saying a quick prayer to whatever gods were watching that the gem would not only allow him to pass, but the dog as well, he looked at the wall. He could not believe that this solid wall would soften and allow him to pass. He made a couple of false starts but aborted them just before he hit the wall. Then he had an idea. He turned to face the assembled crowd, waved, and walked backwards so he would not see the stone as he approached it.

The mist surrounded him and the faces of the people in the cave faded. He turned as soon as they disappeared and checked to make sure Cledo was still with him. He found himself face to face with a very startled young couple.'Where did you come from?' queried the young man. 'I didn't see you up here when we got here.'

'Oh, I've only just arrived. I came up the steep way. Better exercise, you know.'

There was a way up to the standing stones that entered through the arch Pettic came through but people rarely used it, being a rather stiff climb. Also many legends and myths surrounded the stones, many telling of dangers, fairies abducting folk to their land and the returning folk finding many years had passed since they left. There were also tales of dragons and other strange beasts being seen in the stones. They were said to have come through the very arch that Pettic now came, and that was another reason not to enter that way. Who knew what one might meet either in the arch or its immediate vicinity.

Pettic apologised to the couple and told them he would leave them and began the walk down to the city. He shivered. It felt cold here after the heat of Terra.

First he had to go to the home of the family that was looking after Cledo. The children squealed in delight to have the dog back, and Cledo greeted them enthusiastically so Pettic did not feel quite so bad at leaving him.

'Did your business go well,' inquired Nontid, the stable hand.

'Yes,' Pettic said. 'Very successfully thank you .'

He left the dog and set off for the palace. He entered by the stable door because he did not want to draw attention to his return, especially not from Torren. He would prefer not to meet the impostor at all, but he supposed he would have to eventually. He knew he was being a coward, but who knew what reaction Torren would have to his absence. He had not even found out how long he had been gone. Not years, certainly, but was it days, months? It was still winter here, but winter of which year?

Chapter 9

He found out long he had been gone fairly quickly. As he passed Lucenra's rooms her door opened and the princess came out. She stopped in her tracks when she saw Pettic and then grinned.

'Pettic!' she exclaimed. 'I'm pleased to see you back. It hasn't been long though. I thought it would take longer than a week to find the gem.'

Pettic grinned to hear the time had passed slower here than in the world of Terra and told Lucenra so. She said she had to go to see her father and would be back soon. She told Pettic to go and wait in her rooms as she was anxious to hear his story.

Pettic stood in the princess's rooms looking at the portrait of her parents that stood over the fireplace. It was a cold day and he walked over to the hearth and held his hands out to the blaze. After a few minutes he walked over to the window and looked out. Snow still lay on the ground, just as it had when Torren went to meet the mysterious magician in the clearing in the wood. It was turning out to be a hard winter, and Pettic shivered, remembering the heat of the world he had just come from.

How would Klondor have reacted to this cold? he wondered.

Just then the door opened and Lucenra returned. She closed it behind her and went to warm her hands at the fire. She wore a blue dress trimmed at the neck and cuffs with the fur of a fox. She pushed her hands into the sleeves. Although the fire kept the living area of the princess's apartment warm, moving about the corridors was cold.

After getting warm, Lucenra walked over to the window and stood looking out next to Pettic.

'It was hot there,' he said, without looking at his companion. 'Far hotter than it ever is here. I had to wear a white robe most of the time or be cooked.'

'Was it Igni, then, that you arrived in?'

'No! Strangely enough, this hot place was Terra. It was very similar to here, but the people seemed much more primitive.'

'Tell me all about it, please,' Lucenra said, moving to a seat and patting the space next to her to encourage Pettic to sit too. He left the window and went to sit next to her. As soon as he sat he began his tale, starting with his arrival in the cave, and ending with his return through the cave wall.

Lucenra listened in amazement at the tale, then Pettic lifted the sword and showed her the emerald in its hilt.

'My earring is still warm when I'm near it,' he told her. 'I wondered if it would stop reacting once I was back here. Not that there's any reason it should, though is there? That was an irrational supposition on my part.'

'We must take this sword to Blundo as soon as we're able,' Lucenra said. 'I think it would be better left with him, too, for safe-keeping. We don't want Torren to get wind of what we're doing. He'd no doubt steal any or all of the artefacts if he knew.'

'If Blundo's right, then he'd only need to take one. All four are needed to get into the Bubble.'

Lucenra asked many questions about Pettic's adventure, especially about the whirlwind courtship and betrothal of Klondor and Beline.

'I wish I could have known her,' she said. 'And Klondor too, of course. They both sound wonderful people. And to be always summer. How marvellous! I hate winter. I suppose if it's always warm there's no need for them to build stone houses for warmth.'

'No. Their houses are built to keep the heat out. They have no windows at all, only a doorway, which is closed by a bead curtain. The curtain is held back during the day to let some light in, but the huts are surprisingly cool with no windows to let in the heat.'

They talked on for some time, Pettic wanting to know what had happened in the week he had been away.

'I think mother and father are beginning to notice something about Torren,' the princess told him. 'He behaves well enough around them, but some whispers have been getting through, I think. Father sent for Torren a few days ago. I think the Duke of Kroldor complained to Father about that game of cards you and Torren were playing with his daughter and her friend. He went home in a huff, anyway.'

Pettic put his head in his hands. 'I tried to stop the game, Lucenra, really I did, but Torren was having none of it. I really had little choice.'

The princess placed a hand on his arm.

'I know you wouldn't have humiliated those girls voluntarily, Pettic,' she said quietly. 'I only hope Torren didn't decide to put the blame on you. That's the sort of thing this Torren would do, you know.'

'Yes, I suppose he would.' Pettic sighed. 'Would your father have believed him if he had?'

'I don't know, Pettic. I wish I did.'

Pettic went back to his own apartment and sat down. Lucenra had told him she would come later to see Blundo. Pettic found the valet the king had given him checking through his clothes and putting those that needed cleaning onto the bed.

'My Lord,' bowed Larro, 'I'm pleased to see you back. Was your business successful?'

'Yes, thank you, Larro. Most successful. Have my parents written while I was away? I'm anxious to see how they're getting on at the castle. I won't be able to go for some time and I'm a bit concerned about them.'

'Yes, My Lord,' replied, Larro. 'The letter's there on the mantle.' With that he continued to sort through the clothes.

Pettic opened the letter. His mother, it seemed, had taken to being Lady of the Manor, or should we say Castle, as though born to it.

But then again, she was always bossing me about, so a few more folk don't seem to faze her at all, wrote his father.

The letter went on to talk about the stock and how many animals there were and the harvest, which animals his father had chosen to slaughter for the winter and which to keep as breeding stock for next year.

Pettic smiled on reading that his parents had managed to take on this new role. It was not so very different from running their own farm except in scale. There was also a steward to help his father and a housekeeper to help his mother.

He decided to send for his brother to come to court as soon as this business was over so he could learn something of the ways of the nobility. After all, he was an earl's brother, and currently his heir.

Pettic sent for some food in his room. He did not yet want to meet Torren. He thought that the false prince might decide something very unpleasant for him since he had been away without telling him. Perhaps for the next trip he should tell Torren something. Make up a reason for a visit to his castle. After all, he'd not actually been there since his parents moved in.

Just then a knock came at the door. Pettic's valet opened it and announced 'Her Royal Highness, the Princess Lucenra.'

The said Royal Highness entered and went up to Pettic.

'I think we can go now,' she told him. 'We've finished luncheon and my father's busy with kingly things. Mother's going to see the Duchess of Hemmling and Torren's going out with his new guard friends. The other children are in the nursery with Nanny.'

The pair set off to the tower. After climbing the many stairs, they came to the magician's door. Pettic knocked and Blundo's apprentice. admitted them. As soon as he saw who it was, Blundo excused his apprentice, telling him he could have the rest of the day off. The young man quickly ran down the stairs as though he thought his master might change his mind.

'So you've returned, I see. Did you get the gem?' he said.

Pettic showed him the sword. Blundo then wanted to know all about the world of Terra and how Pettic found the sword.

'A world without magic?' he exclaimed when Pettic told him. 'How can that be? It's hard to think of living without magic.'

He listened carefully to all Pettic had to say on the subject of the world of Terra, exclaiming every so often. Lucenra listened carefully for the second time and seemed as interested as before.

'We thought it would be best if you kept the sword,' Pettic said to the magician. 'It'll be safer here than in my apartment. Few people would dare steal from a magician.'

Blundo readily agreed, and taking the sword he put it in a cupboard and locked it with magic. Then Lucenra and Pettic descended the stairs and left the tower.

Just as they passed the end of the corridor leading to the stables, who should come striding towards them dressed for riding, but Prince Torren.

'Pettic,' he called. 'You didn't tell me you were back. Why not?'

'He's only just got here, Torren,' lied Lucenra. 'I met him just a second ago as I was passing.'

'Well he's here now. I was just going riding. Come on, turn round and come with me. Your horse must need exercise. He's not been out in over a week.'

Lucenra turned to her brother. 'Pettic has just got back. Don't you think you should give him time to rest before he goes out again?'

Torren was about to round on his sister when Pettic stepped in. 'It's fine, Lucenra,' he told the girl. 'It's true that Mistro needs exercise. I'll go with the prince. I'm not too tired.'

Lucenra was about to argue when she saw the look in her brother's eyes so she turned away and continued down the passage towards the comfort of the nursery where she had been so happy as a child.

The ride was not as bad as Pettic had expected. Torren did not abuse his horse and seemed to genuinely enjoy the ride. He was almost pleasant to Pettic and they rode for quite a distance away from the city.

Once out in the countryside, Torren suggested a race. The two young men galloped across the hillside neck and neck, until eventually they reached the point designated as the winning post—a large dead oak tree. The prince just won by a neck and laughingly dismounted to walk his sweating horse in circles to cool her down. Pettic followed suit and the old camaraderie Pettic and the real Torren had felt almost returned.

Was this truly the usurper? Could Prince Torren have somehow escaped and returned? Pettic frowned, but then he remembered. The king had given Torren a dressing down about his behaviour so he was probably trying to be more like the real prince.

After walking their horses to cool them down, they set off back to the city at a walk. On the way, Torren began to ask Pettic about the business he had been on in the week he was away. So like was this Torren to the original in looks, and now he was behaving more like a normal human being that Pettic almost told him of his excursion to the world of Terra and only just stopped himself.

He thought quickly and told his companion that he had been looking at a bull he was thinking of buying to improve the stock at his castle. They rode along discussing the merits of various animals.

This was not something Torren had ever discussed with him. The Prince had no experience of raising stock and could not talk about it. This young man in Torren's likeness had obviously been on a farm for quite some part of his life. Pettic actually enjoyed the ride back to the city, to his surprise.

When they returned to their apartments Torren told Pettic that he would expect him at dinner with the rest of the family that evening. Pettic, he said, had been a part of the family for many years and had always eaten with them, and he expected no difference now. Pettic smiled and said he would be there.

That evening, when they had finished eating, the king summoned Pettic to his private office. There he sat down behind his desk and began to speak severely.

'I had a complaint about your conduct just before you went away,' said the king. 'It was to your rooms that two innocent young ladies came for a game of cards with you and Prince Torren. I understand that you suggested a game of strip poker. I also understand that the young ladies objected, but you insisted, even threatening them if they did not comply, saying you would use your influence with the Crown Prince to somehow make their lives a misery.'

Pettic opened his mouth to speak and say it was Torren who made the suggestion and the threats, but decided it would avail him nothing. The king continued.

'Then, as I understand it, half naked, the young ladies fled the apartment leaving you and Torren almost fully clothed. They had never played poker before and the pair of you were, if not experts, then certainly not novices. Yes, I know about your trips to the guardhouse when you were younger.'

The king stood and began to pace the room.

'This behaviour is not to be tolerated. Yes, Torren could have stopped this, but he didn't. He went along, and he has been duly punished, but as the ringleader you must bear the greater share of the blame, and therefore the punishment. I'm surprised at you, Pettic. I would not have put you down as a young man to take advantage of young girls. I'm banishing you to your castle until further notice.

That is the worst misdemeanour, but there is another thing. Your dog. That wolfhound attacked my son. According to Torren he has been growling at him for some time now. Torren says he can't understand it because the animal knows him well and usually greets him almost as enthusiastically as he greets you. He has obviously become a dangerous animal. It sometimes happens. I order him to be put down.'

King Horraic sat down.

'Do you have anything to say for yourself?' he asked.

Pettic looked at the king wide-eyed. He could not say anything against the prince. The king would not believe him, and as for Cledo, well, it was true that the wolfhound had been growling at Torren and had attacked him. What was more, his dog was innocent, but there was nothing he could say to prove it. The order of the king was more potent than the threat made by Torric. Pettic had no doubt he would carry out his orders as soon as possible.

'When am I to go, your majesty,' Pettic asked in a quiet voice.

'Pack up your things tonight and leave first thing tomorrow. I will sort out the destruction of your dog. Now leave us.'

Pettic left the king's office and turned towards his rooms. He had until the next morning and he had to see Lucenra. Her rooms were on the next corridor to his. He knocked on her door. After a few minutes one of her ladies opened it.

'Oh, Earl Pettic,' she exclaimed. 'I'll go and tell her Highness you're here. Please wait in the antechamber.'

The apartment was bigger than Pettic's, as befitted a princess. She had an antechamber for guests to wait in until she could see them, and also a dining room as well as a drawing room. Her maid had a room to herself and the garderobe was in Lucenra's rooms too so she did not have to leave to relieve herself, unlike Pettic who used the one at the end of the corridor.

After a few minutes Lucenra appeared.

'Come into my drawing room, Pettic. We need to discuss what to do next.'

'I'm afraid there's a problem, Lucenra,' said Pettic. 'I've been banished until further notice. Tomorrow morning I'm to go to my castle.'

Lucenra looked at Pettic incredulously. 'Why?' she said. 'You've done nothing to warrant that.'

'It seems Torren put the blame on me for the incident with the two girls. He said it was all my idea. Then he told the king that Cledo had attacked him, and the king has ordered him to be put down.'

'That's terrible, Pettic. Didn't you tell my father the truth?'

'How could I? Your father obviously believed Torren's story. He would have thought that I was making it up to save myself. That would have only made it worse.'

Lucenra stood up and walked to the window. It was quite dark now and the lights from the palace glistened on the snow where it had not been trampled into mud by the people going about their business. She pulled the curtains together and turned.

'What are we going to do about getting the next artefact?'

'I don't know, ' replied Pettic. 'I can't come back here to go through the stones without risking arrest. Can you find someone else you trust to take on the quest?'

'Not really. I don't think we should tell anyone else. The fewer people who know about this the better. More people in the know will increase the risk of Torren finding out what we're up to.'

'Then I'll have to come back then. If I get here after dark and go straight to the stones it should be safe enough. No one goes there at night.'

'What about Cledo?'

'I'll take him with me. If your father looks for him and can't find him he'll suspect I've taken him, but it'll be too late. I can't let him kill Cledo. He's innocent of any wrongdoing.'

They agreed Pettic would return under cover of darkness at the next full moon. and go straight to the standing stones to pass into, hopefully, another world.

Aeris

Chapter 10

Pettic's parents were pleased to see him when he returned to them. He helped them as much as he could while he was there. He was pleased to see that his father's letter had been accurate and his mother was not worried at all about having charge of a number of servants. In all truth, the housekeeper helped her more than a little until she got used to issuing orders for things she used to do herself.

The farming side of running the estate was also going well under his father, who was delighted to have so many hands to help. Having farmed himself, his father was much more knowledgeable than the previous earl and they appreciated being able to talk about what they were doing with him.

Pettic's brother, Derkil, however, pestered him endlessly about when he could go to court. The sixteen year old thought even living in the luxury of Pettic's castle was nothing compared to the luxury of the court.

Pettic became weary of it when the time came for him to leave. He told his brother he would send for him as soon as he could, but that he was not returning to the palace just yet. He had an errand to perform for the Princess Lucenra. No, he did not know just how long it would take. It may be days, but it equally may be many months. He refrained from saying that it could even be years.

Pettic considered leaving Cledo behind at his castle, but in the end he decided to take the dog. The king may have been looking for the animal and he would quickly have come to the conclusion that Pettic had spirited him away to the castle. Also, the dog was company. He had been lucky in the realm of Terra inasmuch as he had found a companion and friend, but who knew if that would happen again.

Pettic left his family and made his way to the capital city. He travelled at night whenever possible so as to not be seen and recognised. He also took by-roads whenever possible and arrived at the standing stones on the night of the full moon, as planned.

As he approached the stones and entered into the circle. A figure stepped out from next to one of them. Cledo bounded over to it and gave an enthusiastic greeting and Pettic realized it was Lucenra.

'What are you doing here?' he exclaimed.

'I can't let you go off to realms unknown without saying goodbye to you. Who knows how long it will be before you re-turn? And I've missed seeing you around the palace.'

I've missed seeing you, too, Lucenra. I'm glad you came here to see me off, just like last time. I only hope the time is similar, or not much longer than the visit to Terra.'

He glanced at the stones and saw the moon rising towards them.

'It looks as though it's nearly time. I must go.'

The princess, as she did before, stood on tiptoe and kissed him on the cheek.

'Good luck,' she whispered, and stepped back to watch as Pet-tic and Cledo stepped through the arch and into the rays of the full moon.

'See you whenever,' he said as he stepped into the mist that once more swirled around him.

He emerged into a bright light and found himself walking through an arch into a beautiful garden. Pettic looked up and saw what appeared to be a glass dome above him through which the sun shone in an impossibly blue sky. He frowned, wondering why the dome was there.

He saw a man with a long black cloak hurrying towards him and stopped to wait until he arrived. As the man got nearer, Pettic saw, to his surprise, that the person approaching was not wearing anything other than the cloak.

'Who are you?' demanded the man when he got near enough. 'How have you managed to get into the Royal Gardens?' Which city are you from? You aren't from here or I'd know you.'

Pettic wrinkled his brow not knowing how to answer these questions.

'You'd better come with me. We can't have just anyone entering here. And we need to find out how you got in.'

Pettic thought he'd better answer the man's questions as best he could.

'I'm from another dimension,' he said. 'I walked between some standing stones at full moon and it brought me here to this garden.'

The man snorted. 'A likely story. Come with me and we'll see what the boss has to say.'

Pettic followed the man to a large ornate building at the far end of a long lawn. He took Pettic round the side and entered a door. This led into a room with a long table down the centre with papers scattered over it. A large man sat at the far end reading some of the papers.

Pettic and his captor stood waiting for several minutes until the large man cast his small eyes over the pair.

'What have you brought me now?' he snapped.

'Found him in the garden, sir. Just walked through the archway into the rose garden.'

'Well, why haven't you taken him straight to the prison? He's obviously one of the groundlings, although how he got up here I'd like to know.'

The man stood up and walked round the table. Pettic noticed that he too wore a long cloak and nothing else, but his cloak was a bronze colour.

'Well, how did you get here?' demanded the man, who was obviously in charge.

'I'm from another dimension. I stepped into an arch in some standing stones when the full moon was shining through and found myself here.'

The large man snorted as he walked round Pettic.

'A likely story. Another dimension indeed. Everyone knows it's not possible to travel to other dimensions.' He reached out his hand and grabbed Pettic's arm. As he did so there was a growl from Cledo and he pulled it back quickly, but not before Pettic had noticed that what he had thought of as a cloak was attached at hand and ankle and seemed to be some kind of membrane.

'Raise your arms,' the man demanded.

Pettic lifted his arms to the sides.

'See, sir,' said his captor. 'No membrane. He must be a groundling. And he's wearing clothes. Only the groundlings wear clothes.'

The other man looked sharply at the man in black.

'Sir,' he added as an afterthought.

'So it would seem. What's this creature next to him that seems so fierce?'

'It's called a 'dog',' Pettic replied.

'What's it for?'

'He's a companion, a guard and a friend. He also helps me when I'm hunting.'

'Take him away. He can do for the next time Her Majesty wants to be entertained.'

Pettic found himself being led away towards another building. Here the guard thrust him into a small room with bars at the door and window.

He sat down on a bench that ran along one side of the cell, for cell it was. Stroking Cledo, he sighed.

'A nice pickle we're in, boy. I wonder what the entertainment for Her Majesty might be? Since it seems to involve prisoners I doubt it's anything good for us.'

Cledo whined in answer and settled down at Pettic's feet.

Hours passed. No one came near. Pettic talked to his dog, glad for the company.

'Somehow we need to get out of here. We need to find the gem in this place. I surmise that it's somewhere near here, but my earring isn't indicating it's close.'

He stood and walked to the door of the cell, then back to the seat. Cledo pricked up his ears, listening to his master.

'On Terra and Ignis we arrived somewhere I could get to the gem, so I think the same would apply here.'

He continued to think. He decided they must have arrived on Aeris. It couldn't be Aqua as there was little or no sign of water. The membranes that seemed to grow from the arms of the residents implied they could, if not fly, at least they could glide.

Several days went by. They fed Pettic, and after a few questions about what Cledo would eat, they gave the dog food as well.

'They don't mean us to die of starvation, Cledo,' Pettic told his companion. 'At least they're giving us adequate food and drink. It's not bad for prison food either.'

The guards changed daily. One did the day shift and another the night. Pettic noticed the night guard slept much of his watch, only waking periodically to check on Pettic.

The day guard seemed a little more talkative than the other, and Pettic asked him what was going to happen to him.

'Well,' mused the guard, who said his name was Gramno, 'I expect they'll take you to the court and try you. Depending on what happens, there are several outcomes.

'You could be cast from the city, and as you've no means of gliding, you'd fall to the ground and be killed.'

'What do you mean, "Fall to the ground?" '

'It's a long drop. We could fly higher if they want to make sure you die, or they could fly lower if they just want you to be crippled.'

Pettic's mind was whirling. He was beginning to understand what was going on here.

'Are you telling me this city can move up and down through the air?'

The guard looked startled. 'Well yes, of course. And travel around too. Where've you been that you don't know that? Every little schoolkid, and even those younger than that know the cities fly.'

Pettic sighed. 'I've told you. I'm not from Aeris. I come from another dimension. My world is called Fusionem and is, like, an amalgamation of the other four dimensions, Terra, Ignis, Aeris and Aqua. That's why I don't know anything about your world.'

Gramno laughed, 'A fertile imagination, you have. I like you, in spite of you being a groundling.'

'Please explain what a groundling is. People keep on saying that I'm one, and it seems to be something bad, but no one has said exactly what one is.'

'You're still keeping it up then, that you're from this Fusionem place? OK, then, I'll humour you.' He dragged his chair closer to the bars and sat on it

'A groundling is a person born without the membrane. They're not allowed to live in the cities but are banished to the ground below. Here they grow our food and make whatever goods we in the cities need.'

'Why are they banished?'

'How should I know? They're deemed unworthy to live here, or even to enter the cities. They creep on the ground below and serve we who live in the cities. That's all I can tell you.'

Pettic had a thousand and one questions he wanted to ask, but Gramno turned away.

Several days passed before Pettic heard anything and then Gramno took him to a large room where a guard thrust him unceremoniously into a cage at one side of the room. Seats filled back of the room and these were filling with people.

All had the same membranes as the people he had already seen, but there were different colours. There were no black ones in the crowd but there were red, grey, white, and a few silver, gold and copper as well as a scattering of bronze. Everyone seemed to have hair the same colour as their membranes. The silver and gold occupied the seats at the front and the copper and bronze behind. The others were at the back.

A door at the side opposite the cage opened and three people entered, two men and a woman. Each had silver membranes and silvery hair. They took their seats at a table on a platform. Another person entered and sat at a desk just below the platform. She lifted a gavel and thumped it on the desk.

'All rise for Her Highness, the Princess Eloraine,' she said, fitting her actions to her words.

Everyone in the court, for Pettic deduced that he was here for his trial, rose and looked towards the door. It opened and the princess entered, flanked by four black-membraned guards.

Pettic drew in a quick breath. She was beautiful. Quite the most beautiful girl he had ever seen. She had long golden hair that almost matched her golden membranes. He could not help but notice her figure, unaccustomed as he was by the nudity with which he was surrounded.

She had small, but perfectly shaped breasts and long slim legs. Her stomach was flat and her narrow waist seemed to emphasise her breasts and hips.

When he finished looking at her figure, Pettic looked at her face. She had large brown eyes with the longest lashes he had ever seen. Her nose was small and upturned and she had a generous mouth that looked as if it liked to smile. Now, however, it was serious.

The Princess walked to the platform where the three people had gone previously. She waved a hand at them and one of them rushed to bring her a chair. She had him place it in the centre of the table that graced the platform. The other judges shuffled up to make room for her. The princess then sat, waving to everyone in the court to do the same.

When everyone was seated and had settled down, the Princess rose.

'I have decided, with my mother's permission, to take control of this trial. I will choose the punishment if the defendant is found guilty, although I think that his innocence will be hard to prove. He is, after all, a groundling. That can't be hidden. Let the trial commence.'

One of the three people on the platform with Princess Eloraine stood and stepped down from the platform and walked over to the cage where Pettic stood. She walked round looking him over.

'Let him be naked as we are,' she said. 'How can we judge if he's truly a groundling if we can't see properly if he has a membrane or not. Sometimes aerials are born with a small membrane. Then they are not considered to be true groundlings.'

Pettic hesitated. The black-membraned guard on his left hissed at him

'Do as the councillor says,' he said. He poked a prod through the bars and as it struck Pettic, he felt an excruciating pain.

He removed his clothes reluctantly in front of so many people.

A gasp rose from the assembled crowd. It seemed they had not seen a groundling before. At least, not one standing naked before them.

Pettic discovered from Gramno that it was customary for groundlings to wear clothes as it was often cool on the surface of the planet. The cities were heated and so the aerials found it acceptable to go naked. Anyway, wearing clothes would be difficult with their membranes. Any that were worn would hamper the use of them in gliding from one building to another, or from one city to another.

The trial continued. Another of the judges, as Pettic had come to think of them, came down and inspected him.

'Raise your arms,' he commanded.

Pettic did so.

'No sign of a membrane. He's definitely a groundling.'

He returned to his seat and the third judge, or councillor, as the guard called him, came to look at Pettic. He took a quick look and declared he too considered the young man to be a groundling. He returned to his seat.

The woman seated at the desk then rose.

'All the judges are in agreement. The prisoner is a groundling who has come to the city illegally. Princess Eloraine will now pronounce sentence.'

Pettic came to the front of the cage and called out to the people in the court.

'This is not justice. I've not been allowed to state my case. I arrived here from another dimension using magic. I didn't choose where I arrived, the magic did. I demand to be allowed to speak.'

A murmur arose from the crowd. The woman at the desk rose.

'Silence,' she shouted, although it was unclear whether she was talking to the crowd or Pettic. 'A groundling does not have the right to speak in this courtroom.'

She spoke to Pettic this time. 'You will listen to Princess Eloraine's sentence.'

She sat down and the princess rose to her feet.

'I know groundlings have no rights,' she said, 'but I'm interested in what this one will say if it has permission. Therefore I grant it the right, in this instance to speak.'

Pettic looked round. The councillors looked angry, as did some of the crowd, but most were interested at this change in protocol.

He began to speak.

'I come from the world of Fusionem. It lies in the centre of the four elemental worlds of Terra, Ignis, Aeris and Aqua and seems to be a fusion of all four elements. This is why it's called Fusionem.' He looked round the assembled people, then at the princess.

'I live in the land of Ponderia. We have a King and Queen and they have several children. The eldest will be King in his turn when the present King dies. The eldest child of King Horaic is Crown Prince Torren.'

At this point, one of the councillors said, 'Get on with it. We don't need to know all of this. You're guilty, and making up fanciful stories won't get you anywhere.'

Princess Eloraine held up her hand.

'Let him continue,' she said. 'I enjoy a good story. He'd make a good writer, I think, if he can tell as good a tale as this one.'

Pettic looked at the princess. 'Thank you, Your Highness,' he said. Then he continued with his tale.

'Torren and I have been good friends since we were thirteen years old. I lived in the palace and was educated with the royal children.

'Suddenly, Prince Torren seemed to be behaving oddly. He was cruel where he had once been kind, he was thoughtless where he had been considerate and he was selfish where he had been generous. His sister, Princess Lucenra, noticed this too and also that Torren was leaving the palace occasionally on his own.'

Pettic coughed.

'I followed him one day and found out he wasn't Torren at all, but another young man. This young man was spelled to look like Torren. I saw a magician enchanting a ring that Torren wore. This ring's magic made the other young man look just like Torren.

'Lucenra and I visited the castle's magician and he told us it was possible Torren had been kidnapped and imprisoned in what he called 'A Bubble of Reality.' That's a mini-dimension created by the wizard.

'The only way to enter that bubble was by finding four gems hidden in the Elemental Worlds. I found the gems belonging to Terra and Ignis, an emerald and a ruby, and I'm here to find the gem of Aeris.'

At the end of his tale, the audience burst into spontaneous applause.

'The crowd enjoyed your tale, anyway,' said the woman councillor. 'but they're easily pleased.'

'Madam,' replied Eloraine looking down her pretty nose, 'I enjoyed it too. This young man has a brilliant imagination.'

The woman councillor huffed and was silent.

The princess then stood.

'Do any of you councillors now think Pettic is innocent, and has come to the city by accident?'

All the councillors shook their heads, although the younger of the two men seemed to hesitate and look at the others first.

'I would like to spare you, Pettic,' Eloraine said, 'but unfortunately all the councillors have decided you are a groundling and I must abide by that decision. However, I won't condemn you to being cast off the city. We'll take you and your ... dog, is it? and put you on the ground in a place where no other groundlings live. It's a dangerous place with many wild beasts that will hunt you.'

She looked at Pettic. He felt embarrassed at his nakedness and blushed. the princess smiled.

'If you survive I will allow you to come back to the city and be my pet groundling.'

There were gasps of horror at this. Although there had been aerials with pet groundlings before, it had not happened for centuries and the current people thought them little more than animals and not fit to live in one on the flying cities.

No one objected, however. Princess Eloraine had passed her verdict. She would be queen when the current queen died. It would not do to upset her.

Gramno took Pettic back to his cell to wait his transport to the surface of Aeris.

Three days later, guards came and led Pettic from his cell, along with Cledo, to the edge of the city. A door opened in the dome and he looked down at the ground below. He felt dizzy. He was higher than he had been riding Monarlisk.

As he looked, the ground seemed to be coming nearer and he realised the city was slowly descending.

'How does this work?' he asked one of his guards.

'The court magicians are doing something in that tower.' He pointed to a tower rising above all the other buildings. 'Don't' ask me what. If I knew that. I'd be a magician myself.'

During his time in the cell, Perric had got to know his guards quite well and they liked him. '*Not bad for a groundling,*' one of them had said. '*Quite bright for one of them, too, Almost as bright as an aerial, though only a red, of course.*'

Pettic had found out the aerials had a strict hierarchy. The groundlings, with no flight membranes, were the lowest of the low and treated as animals They lived on the ground and were the labouring class.

Of those with membranes, the reds were the lowest class and the gold the highest, followed by silver and bronze. The blacks were always guards or soldiers.

A guard handed him a backpack containing a wooden bowl, a flask of water and a spoon. He noticed that at the bottom of the pack was some dried meat and a few dried vegetables. They wouldn't last long though. He'd need to hunt.

'Just a few provisions for you to get you going,' the guard told him.

Suddenly there appeared a glint of gold in the sunlight. Pettic looked and saw three gold-winged figures gliding from a tower to land gracefully near where he was standing.

'Well, Pettic,' said Princess Eloraine, for it was indeed she and two of her siblings, 'are you ready?'

'As ready as I'll ever be,' he grunted.

'Take his sword and give him the dagger and then take them down,' Eloraine told two of the guards who we're waiting nearby with some kind of harness.

The princess smiled at the young man. 'Good luck,' she said and turned away to talk to her brother and sister.

The guards approached Pettic and Cledo and began to strap on the harnesses. The dog objected both to himself being strapped in and to Pettic also. He growled at the guards as they approached.

'Down, Cledo,' Pettic said, and at that word, Cledo allowed himself to be strapped into the harness that was then attached to a guard. Pettic was likewise strapped to another guard.

Suddenly, a man came running from the city.

'Please wait,' he cried. 'My wife has just given birth to a groundling child. Can it go down at this descent?'

The guard took a crying bundle from the man and passed it to Pettic, and at a signal from Eloraine they launched themselves into the air off the side of the city.

Pettic took a deep breath. He heard Cledo whine but then all sound was drowned out by the rushing wind as they descended. The guard had his membranes outstretched and as Pettic was on his back. He could see little. A good thing from his point of view. He did not relish watching the ground rushing up towards them.

It only took a few minutes to reach the ground where the guards unbuckled the harnesses and Pettic and Cledo were free on solid ground.

'How are you going to get back?' Pettic asked the guards.

'Don't worry. They'll haul us up.'

Just then, Pettic became aware of two ropes dangling down from the city above. The guards clipped them to their harnesses and they were unceremoniously hauled up into the sky.

'Well, Cledo, lad, here we are. Our task is to find a village and survive. How will they know? What am I supposed to do with this baby though? I can't leave it here to die, but I have nothing to feed it with.'

As he said this, he noticed a glint as the sun reflected off something.

'Ah, I see. They have telescopes. That's how they'll follow us. But they won't be able to see everything, will they?'

Pettic looked around. They were near the summit of a mountain. A little higher up, snow lay thickly and a little lower down a forest grew. Where they were, between snow and trees, was bare. A few bits of grass struggled to survive in the meagre soil on the mountain, but it was mainly barren rock.

'I suppose any villages will be lower down,' Pettic reasoned, adjusting the baby in his arms.

It had stopped crying for the moment and was asleep.

'That's where we'll head for. Come on. Cledo. This doesn't seem too hard a task after all.'

Pettic spoke too soon, though. Just as they passed a group of loose rocks, something flew out and attacked them. Cledo leaped up and caught the creature just behind its head. His jaws crunched down and it was dead.

Pettic patted the dog. 'Thanks, Cledo. A good job we played all those games of catch on Fusionem.'

The young man then turned to look at what had attacked him.

It appeared to be a snake at first glance but it had wings and what appeared to be feathers, or feather-like scales. The feathers were brightly coloured like some birds, but its head, which was rather large, looked more snake-like, or even dragon-like. Around the head was a ruff that had been spread as the creature attacked.

'What on earth is it?' Pettic asked Cledo, but of course got no reply. He prised open its mouth and saw two large fangs that he had no doubt contained poison.

'Let's cut this head off and see if we can get at the poison sacs,' said Pettic, glad for the companionship of his dog. He thought he would have felt silly talking to himself, but talking aloud definitely made him feel better.

The head was difficult to cut off, but the dagger that Eloraine gave him was sharp and he eventually managed it. Then, with the point of the weapon he probed until he found what he thought were the poison sacs. He carefully cut them out and put them into his pack.

'They might just be useful,' he told the wolfhound. 'Now let's get going.'

Chapter 11

Eloraine and her siblings arrived in the tower in the city. As they entered the room at the top of the structure the chief magician turned to them.

'Did you give him the gem so we can follow his progress?'

'Yes. It's in the dagger I gave him. I had it sent down to the blacksmith in the village near here. He's mounted it in the hilt. Looks quite pretty, actually.'

The magician then turned to the others in the tower with him.

'Right, let's get the resonance going so we can track what he's doing.'

The other three magicians began to chant, and gradually a dot appeared on a map of the land below.

The chief magician picked up four telescopes. He handed one to each of the Royal children and kept one for himself. All four put them to their eyes and looked at Pettic.

Suddenly there was movement behind the young man on the ground and as he span round, his animal—dog he called it—leaped at the attacking creature and caught it behind its head. They could not hear the crunch of bones as the dog's jaws crunched down, but they saw the flying snake flop as it died.

They watched Pettic cut out the poison sacs and put them in his backpack.

Sixteen year old Prince Bramnor looked at his elder sister.

'That's clever. I'd not have thought a groundling would have thought of that.'

His younger sister, thirteen year old Princess Sprinkla, huffed.

'They aren't very clever, Bram, you know that. That's why they're down there working for us instead of enjoying their lives and having fun, like we do.'

'Perhaps this one's different,' mused Eloraine. 'Perhaps he is clever. Maybe he's not like the others.'

Sprinkla looked in amazement at her sister.

'You know groundlings aren't clever. Those born without a membrane can't fly, nor can they reason. That's a known fact. That's why any aerial who has a baby born without a membrane has to send it to the ground. For goodness sake. We've two brothers and a sister down there.'

Bramnor looked at her in disdain.

'We have no brothers and sisters who are groundlings. That's just not possible. Those born to mother were groundlings and not our siblings. We cannot have groundling siblings.'

'Will you two be quiet and watch what the groundling does. That's why we came up here, not to argue,' snapped Eloraine as she turned away and back to her telescope

They watched as Pettic and Cledo began to go down towards the forest, then halt and turn back towards the top of the mountain.

Pettic had indeed decided to go up the mountain. It may be there was a village on the other side. He scanned the land on this side of the mountain and could see no sign of a village, or even any huts to show a possibility of people living there.

They entered the snow-covered part of the mountain. Here the going became difficult. Cledo, especially, found it tough as some of the drifts were almost to the top of his legs. After a time of this, Pettic paused.

'This is no good, Cledo. It'll take us too long to get over this snow. I'm also getting breathless. I think there isn't as much air here. The baby's getting cold too. We'd better go back down to where the snow finishes.'

Matching his actions to his words, Pettic turned and began the trek back downwards, but as he did so he moved diagonally so as to make some progress round the mountain.

A cliff barred his way and he had to move along it. Fortunately he could still continue his downward direction, but then the ground fell suddenly away and he had to turn towards the place where the aerials had left them. Still, the progress was steadily the mountain, so Pettic didn't worry too much about minor obstacles.

Once clear of the snow, Pettic began to move more quickly and soon arrived in the forest. It was beginning to get dark. Pettic had no idea what the season was here on this part of Aeris so had no idea whether it was early or late in the day. He decided they should rest for the night, however long or short it was.

Searching the forest, Pettic found some twigs, dead leaves and larger branches. He had to make a fire, but he had not been given anything to strike a spark with. He remembered that once, when he and Torren had gone off on an expedition, the other boy had made a kind of bow, which he used to start a fire.

Could he make a firebow from what he found in the forest?

Looking around, he spotted a yew tree. He remembered that yew was good for hunting bows. If he used that, he could make himself a bow and some arrows from other trees.

That would be useful. If he had to fight off other creatures, his dagger would not be too useful. He would have to get in too close. Even with Cledo's help it might not be enough. Still, first a firebow.

The baby began to cry again. It must be hungry, but Pettic had nothing to feed it with. He did not even know if it were a boy or a girl, he realised. But first he needed some heat.

Pettic began to search around. First he looked for a couple of sticks. He dug in the ground until he found a root that would be suitable to bind them together. That done, he set about searching for a suitable spindle and wood for a bow.

Once he assembled all the ingredients, he made the bow and dug a hole out of the handplate for the top. Searching for some tinder, he picked up dead leaves and then began to saw away with the point he had made at the end of the spindle in the groove where the two bound sticks met.

In a short time, smoke began to rise and soon he had a little flame. He transferred it to his tinder and blew gently. Gradually he placed small twigs, then slightly larger ones until he had good campfire going.

He took some of the water and put it into a metal container and put it into the flames. He dropped some dried meat and vegetables into it and waited for them to cook. When he had moved the baby, who had gone back to sleep, he passed the time talking to Cledo, who appeared to listen with interest.

After eating and stoking up the fire, Pettic spooned some of the now cool broth into the baby's mouth. It swallowed some of the liquid. Pettic hoped it would be alright. He had no milk for a baby and did not know if broth would upset the tiny stomach. He lay cuddling the baby and preparing to spend a cold night.

He shivered during the night and twice got up to put more wood on the fire, but it did little to warm him. At least not for long. Each time he lay down again, sleep was long in coming.

The next morning, Cledo woke Pettic by licking his face.

'Hey, stop that! I know I probably need a wash, but not like that. I don't need your slobber all over my face.' He wiped his wet face with his sleeve.

The dog stood looking at him as Pettic scrambled to his feet, yawning. Then Cledo wagged his tail as if to say '*That's better. Now you're up we should get going.*'

He started to trot off down a deer track leading in the direction they had been heading the previous night.

'Wait, Cledo,' Pettic called after him. 'I need to tidy up this camp first. Can't leave the fire. It needs putting out completely before we leave here, and I think I'd better give this baby some water. I've no more broth left. Anyway, I need to gather the things I need to make a bow and some arrows.'

Pettic took a clean cloth and dipped it into the water he had filled his water bottle with. The baby sucked hungrily and fell asleep again as its stomach felt full. Pettic knew water would not satisfy it for very long, though. He must find someone to take it over. Someone who could give it the milk it needed.

He searched the forest and soon he found the things he needed. He cut a yew staff and with a makeshift cord, made from some fibrous vine that was growing up a tree, managed to string it. The vine broke several times, but eventually he had a serviceable bow, if not one that was very professional looking.

Then he searched for some straight branches to make arrows. These he sharpened to a point and hardened them in the fire before he put it out, Now he had a bow and a dozen arrows.

He strapped the baby to his back and then they started along the deer path. As they walked, the sun came out and managed to penetrate the trees in places. Suddenly, from ahead, they heard the sound of growls and crashes as if some large beasts fought.

Pettic motioned to Cledo to stay behind him as they crept towards a clearing in the forest. True to the sounds, there was a fight going on. At first, all Pettic could see was a blur, but eventually he noticed some flashes of white.

Every now and again, the creatures separated and looked at each other. One was a beautiful white horse with wings on its back. The other looked something like a dragon, but was much smaller and had only two legs.

After a brief pause, the two ran at each other again. As the dragon-like beast ran at the horse, it reared up, struck the other creature on the head and then batted it with its wings. The dragon-like creature fell over, but jumped up quickly, just before the horse struck it a killing blow with its feet.

Then the horse seemed to slip. It beat its wings to try to steady itself when its opponent struck. It bit hard into the horse's neck and the horse went down. Pettic could not bear to see such a beautiful creature killed. He drew his bow and aimed. When he let fly, Cledo jumped past him and ran to bite the savage dragon-like creature on the leg, hamstringing it.

Pettic's arrow struck the animal in the chest. It did not manage to penetrate far, due to the scaly armour of the beast, but it seemed to decide that the fight was over now new opponents had arrived and it took to the sky and quickly disappeared up into the heights of the mountain.

Pettic approached the horse as it lay on the ground. It was bleeding quite badly from the bite. As luck would have it, the bite had missed any major blood vessels, so Pettic tore a piece of cloth from his shirt and tried to staunch the blood flow.

After a short time, the blood seemed to slow down and Pettic removed the now bloodstained piece of cloth. Sure enough, the wound had almost stopped bleeding. Pettic tied a clean cloth over the wound with some healing herbs he had in his pack and stood back from the animal wondering if he had done the right thing. How would the horse manage to get the bandage off when the wound was healed?

The winged horse looked at Pettic from its soft, brown eyes. It slowly stood and, extending its foreleg, bowed to the young man. Pettic bowed in return. The horse then trotted out of the clearing.

'Well, that was quite an experience, Cledo. A winged horse. Who would have thought it. Of course, this world has magic and so must have magical creatures too. There were dragons on Ignis and so it stands to reason there will be flying creatures on Aeris, but a flying horse? That's something else.'

Just as he finished speaking, he heard a noise from the direction the horse had taken. Pettic raised his bow ready for another creature, but to his surprise it was the horse returning. Behind the creature was a winged foal.

'So that was why she was fighting so hard,' said Pettic to Cledo. 'She was protecting her foal. I expect that other creature, whatever it was. Must have fancied a bit of foal for its breakfast.'

The horse trotted over to Pettic and knelt down. She made to push him with her nose. Pettic did not know what she was trying to do and so he patted her on the neck.

She stood again and then repeated the procedure. Eventually he decided she was telling him he could mount her. He picked Cledo up and tentatively placed him in front of the animal's wings. The horse did not seem to object and so he vaulted onto her back, holding on to Cledo with the crying, and now rather smelly, baby strapped to his back.

The dog whined, remembering how he hated flying on Monarlisk. Pettic soothed him and held him tightly as the horse stood. She trotted out of the clearing, followed by her foal and continued along the track that Pettic and Cledo had been following.

Pettic was a good rider and knew how to control a horse with his knees, but did this horse know the signals? It was obviously not a domesticated beast and had probably never been ridden before.

They came out of the forest into a wide valley. Here the winged horse leaped into the air, followed by her foal. Cledo howled as the ground dropped away.

'Quiet, boy.' Pettic told him. 'I won't let you fall.'

The flight was much smoother than that of the dragon he had ridden before on Ignis, and Pettic found himself enjoying it.

They flew over the valley. A river flowed along the bottom. Pettic used his knees to try to direct the horse to the left so they would follow the valley in the direction he planned to go. They would probably be able to get round to the other side of the mountain, now that they were airborne.

To Pettic's delight, the horse responded. She turned to follow the valley and as it narrowed, she flew higher to avoid the mountains encroaching from either side.

Pettic peered down as best he could over the mare's wings. He could see better in the down sweep and he suddenly saw smoke rising.

That had to be people. Perhaps not a village, as there was only one plume, but if someone were living down there, then perhaps they would know where there was a village. What was more, these people might be able to look after the baby. The child was getting weaker and hardly crying now. Pettic worried about it.

How to get the horse to descent though. Pettic pulled on the mane. The mare began to go higher and so he pushed gently. The mare began to descend. With pushes on her neck and the use of his knees, the mare eventually landed outside a house.

She was obviously not happy at being close to people and as soon as Pettic and Cledo were off her back, she once more bowed to the young man and cantered off, trailed by her foal.

Pettic looked round. The area was farmed, and quite extensively too. The house was quite large and as Pettic walked towards the door, he noticed there were cattle in the fields. The farmers would be able to get milk for the baby.

Around the house, chickens and geese pecked at the ground and he heard the grunting of a pig in a sty around the back.

To one side of the building there was a fenced off area where a variety of plants grew. Pettic could not ascertain what they were, but deduced they must be food plants for the house.

He knocked at the door.

A gruff voice shouted, 'It's not time for you to collect yet. There are still two months growing for the beef to do.'

Pettic called out, 'I'm not here to collect anything. I just want directions to the nearest village.'

The door opened and a man, clad in overalls, came out.

'What do you mean, the nearest village? There ain't a village for miles.'

A female voice came from within the house.

'Joert, tell the aerials the beef ain't ready yet. They're early and they know it. Can't give them beef we ain't got. If they want to punish us, we'll just have to take it.'

'It ain't the aerials, Maoni. It's a groundling just like us. Don't know where he's come from.'

'Let him in then If he's here he must have walked for days.'

The man stood back and let Pettic and Cledo into the house. They entered a passage with doors on each side and stairs going up to the second storey. Joert opened the door on the right and indicated to Pettic that he should enter.

A large dog lying in front of the fire, rose and stalked over to Cledo. Cledo's hackles stood up.

'Quiet, Cledo,' Pettic said in a quiet, calm voice, 'we don't want any fights here and this is his home, after all.'

The other dog sniffed at the newcomer and was sniffed in return. The pair, with a few orders from their respective owners, settled into an uneasy truce. Cledo lay down by the window while the other dog resumed his place by the fire.

Pettic looked round. The room ran the length of the house from front to back and had windows at both ends. There were two chairs with arms, and cushions, embroidered with images of animals and birds on their seats next to the fire. A large table stood at one end of the room surrounded by four chairs and there were cupboards on the other walls.

Joert indicated that Pettic sit on one of the chairs and he pulled out a chair from the table for himself.

'Now, lad,' he said, 'Tell us what you're doing here. If the aerials catch you away from the job you've been given, you'll be punished very severely. Where've you come from? You're not running away are you? No one ever escapes the aerials and if you are they'll put you to death.'

'Yes, I am sort of running away from the aerials, but not because I was one of their slaves.'

Maoni came into the room at that moment and took her place on the other chair by the fire. Picking up some knitting, she looked at Pettic.

'All groundlings are their slaves,' she said. 'No exceptions, and either you're running away or you're not.'

Just then the baby stirred, making a little mewling sound. Maoni stood and looked at the small bundle on Pettic's back.

'It's a baby,' she cried. 'The poor little thing's hungry.'

'Can you feed it?' Pettic replied. 'The aerials sent it down with me. Something about it being born a groundling. I couldn't leave it to die.'

Maoni smiled and took the baby from Pettic's back.

'Of course we can,' she smiled, and she took the child to another room, coming back shortly with a makeshift bottle with milk in it. She sat down and began to feed the child.

When she had settled down, Pettic told the tale of how Prince Torren had been kidnapped and he was trying to find the gems to rescue him. He told of the worlds of Terra and Ignis. His hosts gasped at the story of the dragons and told him that the dragon-like creature he had encountered was a wyvern. It was said be a close relative of dragons, but no one on Aeris really believed in such large, fire-breathing creatures.

Joert balked at the idea of a pegasus, (for that was what he said the flying horse was called) allowing someone to ride on its back. They were shy creatures and shunned human contact.

'He helped the creature and perhaps saved her life and that of her foal,' Maoni told him as she held the baby over her shoulder and gently patted its back. The baby rewarded her with a loud burp. 'She would want to do something in return, I suspect.

Anyway, how else do you explain how he suddenly appeared on our land?'

Joert reluctantly agreed with his wife, then turned to Pettic.

'You say you must reach the nearest village. You were put down near the summit of Mount Etius and from there the nearest village would be Smithtown. That's round the mountain from where they set you down. If you leave here and head westwards, then at the road junction you turn south, you should get there in—what?—five or six days.'

'There are many dangers out there,' Maoni told Pettic 'There are many beasts besides the wyvern and snake that'd have you for their dinner,'. You have your dog, and you have the bow you made, but the arrows aren't very good.' She turned to Joert. 'Do you have any arrows to spare? A few decent ones with a proper metal tip would help him, I'm sure.'

Joert grunted. 'I can spare some, I suppose. The aerials will no doubt have some to trade for the beef.'

'I can't take your arrows. You'll doubtless need them for protecting your animals and crops.'

'Nonsense,' replied Maoni. 'We can't have you going off unprotected. I want to hear no more from you about not taking them.'

Pettic thanked them and then said he should not impinge on their hospitality any longer and that he should be going. The couple looked at one another and an unspoken word seemed to pass between them.

'It's getting near to dark now,' said Joert. 'We would like you to stay the night and eat with us. We can give you some food to take too, and some milk for the baby, although I don't suppose it will last until you reach Smithtown.'

Pettic thanked his hosts. He was certainly not looking forward to another night in the cold. Their generosity moved him greatly and he told them so.

Joert smiled sadly.

'We had a son about your age,' he murmured. 'Until he got to twelve years old. Then the aerials took him. We don't know where they took him, nor to what job they assigned him, but we've not heard anything of him since.'

Maoni was looking into the fire.

'We weren't singled out. It happens to all us groundlings. They come and take our young away to serve them in whatever way they please,' she said. 'It happened to us too. I never saw my parents after I was twelve. They trained me in animal husbandry. That was fine, because I always loved animals. I thought I'd be put on a farm somewhere to rear cattle, sheep or something. Then I was given to Joert as a bride. I didn't know him. I'd never seen him until we were mated. That was the most frightening day of my life. It is for all girls, and I suspect for young men too.'

Joert nodded at this. Maoni turned and smiled at him.

'But I was one of the lucky ones. Joert is a kind man and was gentle with me. They put us on this farm and told us to raise beef for them.

'Joert and I have come to love each other, but that isn't always the case. Many girls I saw as I was growing up ended up with violent men, or men who bullied them in other ways.'

Joert interrupted. 'Then Maoni became pregnant. We were so excited. She gave birth to Bobiam in this house with no one to aid her. She nearly died, but she's a strong woman and she pulled through. However, she could not have any more children and Bobiam was our only one.

'We hoped the aerials would allow him to stay here to take over after us, but they had different plans. One day they came and took him away.'

Joert's voice broke as he spoke and Maoni had tears running down her face. Pettic found he was almost in tears himself at this sad story.

He was angry with the aerials. They obviously thought they were so far above the groundlings that they could treat them as animals. He said as much to the couple.

'Yes, they do,' said Joert.

'Look,' Pettic said, 'You lost your boy. I can't look after this baby. Would you take it and look after it?'

Maoni's eyes filled with tears. 'Would we? We'd love to. By the way, this baby is a little boy. I changed him when I got the milk. Thank you for bringing him to us. I promise we'll take the greatest care of him.'

Pettic was delighted he had found a kind couple to bring up the baby, but there was one thing he wondered about.

'Do the groundlings ever give birth to children with membranes?'

'Sometimes, but not often.'

'What happens to them?'

Maoni had recovered herself by now and she replied, 'They never find any.'

Maoni would say no more and she rose, handed the baby to Joert and began to prepare a meal. Soon there was the smell of a delicious beef stew wafting through the house, and Pettic's stomach began to growl.

After the meal, Pettic helped to clear away and then he fed Cledo with some of the left-over stew Maoni gave him for that purpose. They also gave their own dog some.

The darkness was falling rapidly and Joert showed Pettic to a room at the top of the stairs where he quickly fell into a deep sleep.

The next morning, equipped with two dozen iron-tipped arrows and more food than he thought he would need, Pettic and Cledo said farewell to the friendly couple and began walking westwards as they had directed.

He was not looking forward to a long walk, but he had no choice. He rounded a bend in the road and, to his surprise, standing in the middle was the pegasus mare and her foal. As Pettic approached, she trotted towards him and again, after a bow, knelt down for him to mount.

Pettic smiled at the thought that he did not now have a walk of several days and, hoisting Cledo in front of him, he mounted the horse. With a squeeze of his knees, the mare bounded into the air, followed, of course, by her foal.

They flew westwards until a gap appeared between two mountains to the south. Pettic guided the mare in the direction of the gap and she flew swiftly towards it. As it happened, this was a dead end valley and at the end, the horse began to climb. Cledo, who until that moment had been lying still, front legs on one side of the horse and hind legs on the other, chose that moment to move. As the horse was both changing direction and altitude at the same time, the dog started to slip.

Pettic panicked, but not as much as Cledo. The animal tried to scramble back onto the horse's back while Pettic tried to grab him. The harder Cledo tried to scramble back the more he seemed to slip. Pettic could not seem to get a firm grip on the wolfhound either, and it seemed as if the animal would plunge to his death.

The mare seemed to feel the dog slipping and began to make a rapid descent. She adjusted her direction to try to minimise the slippage as well.

As luck would have it, Cledo finally slipped from the horse's back when they were only about twenty feet from the ground, and although he landed hard, with the breath knocked out of him, he was otherwise unhurt.

When the pegasus touched the ground, Pettic leaped off and ran to his friend.

He felt Cledo all over but could find no broken bones and the dog seemed to be without any pain anywhere.

Pettic looked at the sky. The sun was slipping down in the west and he decided to stay for the night in order to let Cledo recover somewhat before continuing their journey.

The pegasus mare flew off into the distance. Pettic was still unsure of her. Would she come back tomorrow, or would she think her obligation to him was over. After all, she had helped them twice. Perhaps she thought that was enough.

As he gathered wood and lit a fire, Pettic considered his position. This valley was not the one that Joert told him to follow. If the pegasus did not return, then he would have to trek back to the road. How long that would take he had no idea. He had been unable to judge the distance they travelled while flying.

That was a problem for the next day, though and so he collected some water from a nearby stream and settled down to eat some of the beef that Maoni had given him.

He gave some to Cledo who seemed to be fast recovering from his ordeal, much to Pettic's relief, then he checked over his bow and ensured the string was not becoming too dry, and thus too brittle. He decided he should get some more of the vine if he could find it, just in case that string broke.

He spent the next few hours searching until he found plenty of the strong vine and then he and Cledo settled down to sleep.

The following morning, when he awoke, he ate some cheese and bread and then started to put the fire out before leaving.

He looked to the sky. There was no sign of a white creature arriving and he began to think the pegasus had decided not to return. He called to Cledo and they began to walk along a track in the opposite direction from that which they had flown in.

Suddenly he heard a snort from behind some bushes. He reached for his bow but then he saw a familiar head appear over the top of the bushes. It was the pegasus. She came out when she saw Pettic and knelt for him to mount.

Cledo flatly refused to go anywhere near the horse. All the pulling and coaxing would not budge the animal. Pettic sat on the ground to think. Then he had an idea.

He took the new vine he had gathered and wrapped it around Cledo to make a harness. He took another length, longer this time, and he asked permission of the horse to attach it to her. He did not know how much she understood, but it felt right to ask.

It was difficult to get Cledo to go anywhere near the Pegasus. In the end, Pettic had to lift the wolfhound onto the horse's back. This was a difficult job as Cledo struggled the whole of the time in spite of Pettic's soothing words that he would be secure this time.

Once he had the dog across the mare's back, Pettic fastened the two harnesses securely together and then mounted himself.

With a squeeze of his knees, the young man propelled the pegasus into the air and guided her in the direction he wanted to go. Cledo whined the whole of the time, looking over the horse's side at the ground passing beneath him. Soon they were flying over ridges and valleys once more, but never any sign of a village.

After half a day of flying, with Cledo's constant whining getting on his nerves, Pettic guided the flying horse round side of the mountain.

There was a plain on this side and he spotted several plumes of smoke coming from towards the horizon. A village.

Guiding the horse towards the ground, Pettic looked for a road. Sure enough, he spotted one about a mile to the west. He guided the pegasus towards it and got her to land among bushes at the side.

He slipped from her back and released a very relieved Cledo from the harness. On feeling solid ground beneath his feet, the dog began to jump around like a puppy, barking his relief. Pettic went over to the horse and bowed to her. She bowed back and then came towards him and pushed her nose into his shoulder.

He removed the harness, patted her neck and stroked her nose then said, 'Thank you. We wouldn't have got here so quickly without you.'

Then the horse and foal turned, ran a few paces and jumped once more into the air.

Taking to the road, Pettic and Cledo strode the mile or so towards where they saw the smoke rising. Pettic felt rather pleased with himself. He knew the aerials had not expected him to survive, and if he did, that he would not find the village, but here he was. Now they would have to take him back to their flying city where he could begin to look for the gem of this dimension.

The aerials had promised he would be the pet of the Princess Eloraine if he managed this task. What that meant he had no idea, but if he was in the city he could search for the gem and then make his escape.

Chapter 12

Pettic approached the village with caution. It was ringed round with earthworks. Outside the earthworks a ring of sharpened stakes rose and inside the earthworks a moat was fed by a river. This did not look very friendly, but the gate was open and so he carefully entered.

No one stopped him or challenged him on the way through the gates. As he walked down what must be the main street, he noticed almost every building that was not a dwelling was a smith of some sort.

He stopped at the first forge.

'Hello,' he said to the smith who was busy banging a piece of iron on his anvil.

The smith stopped and looked at him.

'Just a moment,' he said as he took the iron and plunged it into a tub of water.

The iron hissed and clouds of steam rose into the air obscuring the smith from view for a few minutes. When the steam cleared he looked at Pettic and frowned.

'Who are you? he asked. 'You don't live in Smithtown. Where've you come from?'

'It's a long story,' Pettic told him.

'You'd better start, then.'

Pettic began to tell the story from the beginning, ending up with his arrival at Smithtown. The smith sighed.

'That's a lot to take in, lad,' he said. 'It's an unbelievable story.'

He looked at Pettic and held up his hand.

'I'm not saying I don't believe you, but it's just not something I've ever heard of before. Still, you did come out of nowhere, aren't an aerial and no groundlings are allowed to leave their village without the aerials' permission, so I guess there must be at least some truth in it.'

'Every word is true,' Pettic told him.

'You look honest, and your eyes are looking straight at me, so I think I believe you. Still, what a story!'

'The aerials told me I was to get to the nearest village and then they'd come down for me. Princess Eloraine said she wants me to be her pet. I don't like the sound of that though.

The smith snorted. 'They'll come down for you, no doubt, but it'll be to hunt you. They like to hunt groundlings.'

Pettic raised his eyebrows. 'They hunt humans?'

'Not in their eyes they don't. We're not humans, see? Something between the animals and the aerials. They consider themselves to be the only true humans.'

Pettic frowned. 'How will they know where I am?'

'Did they give you anything when they brought you down?'

'Yes, this dagger,' replied Pettic.

'Then that's what they'll be using to track you. They've put some magic on it no doubt and can tell where you are at any time. You need to get rid of it. I must get on with this work now. It's for the aerials and they don't like it if the stuff isn't ready.'

He turned his back and picked up the quenched iron again.

As he did so he said, 'There's a tavern down the road. It doesn't have a sign though. Doesn't need one. Everyone here knows where it is and no one else comes.'

Pettic wandered out of the forge and down the main street. It seemed every building was a forge of some kind. Not all were blacksmiths. There were a few whitesmiths as well, working with pewter, and he even saw a silversmith or two and a gold-smith.

'*So that's why it's called Smithtown,*' he thought. '*All the smiths in one town. I wonder if that's the same in other towns too?*'

Eventually he came to a house situated between a whitesmith and a silversmith. He had seen no other houses and so he de-cided this must be the tavern. He opened the door and entered.

It was indeed the tavern. It comprised one large room with a number of barrels at one end. Several tables were scattered around and a few men sat with tankards of ale in front of them. They all stared at Pettic and Cledo as they entered.

'What can I do for you?' asked a large man, getting up from where he had been sitting talking to three men.

'I was hoping for a drink,' Pettic answered, 'but I don't have any money.'

'Money? We don't use money here,' the large man replied. 'The aerials don't allow us money.'

'Then how do you make a living?'

The men, who were talking to the large man, laughed.

'We give something in return,' one of them told him. 'What've you got?'

'Anyhow,' said another, 'how come he don't know that? He's a groundling ain't he?'

Pettic gave a brief explanation, simply telling them he had come from another dimension and been condemned to the ground.

'You'se a groundling, though,' said another, older man who was missing several teeth. 'So this is where you should be. The aerials won't leave you be, though.'

'So I've heard. They gave me this dagger. I'd like to get rid of it. Would you like to trade it for a tankard of ale?'

'No.' The answer was adamant from all of them.

'I haven't got anything else. They took my sword.'

'What about that earring? That'd look good on my wife, it would.'

'Or that amulet round your neck,' said another.

Pettic sighed. He couldn't get rid of either of the two magic items. The earring was how he knew he was near to the gem and the amulet was what allowed him to understand and be understood.

He decided he'd have to explain the whole thing to them.

After telling the story, he removed his amulet. Immediately the speech around him became incomprehensible. He spoke to the men and they wrinkled their brows. He replaced it and everyone could understand each other again.

The men seemed to believe him, if a little reluctantly. The fat man, who seemed to be the tavern owner, dipped a ladle into one of the barrels and filled a tankard.

Handing it to Pettic, he said, 'The story was a good one, and it might be true. You've earned your drink. What about your dog?'

Pettic asked for some water and the innkeeper duly served Cledo too.

One of the men at the table leaned across to Pettic. 'I might be able to help you with yon dagger,' he said, nodding in the direction of the said article. 'I've an idea.'

Pettic followed the man out of the back of the tavern. They walked through the village, past some residential houses, until they came to the earthworks. Here they sat by the side of the moat.

Cledo sniffed the air, then settled down to wait. Soon, a dark shadow appeared in the water that filled the ditch below the earthworks. Slowly, the man slithered down and lay close to the edge. He slipped his hand into the water and carefully moved it towards the large shadow, waving his fingers as though they were fronds of reeds. Then, quick as a flash, he whipped his hand into the air and a large shape came flying out.

Pettic caught the large fish. It was long and slender and very slippery.

'Don't drop it,' called his companion. 'It can slither back into the water in a flash.'

Pettic struggled with the creature but managed to hang on to it until the other man came up. Between them, and with difficulty, they took the dagger and strapped it onto the fish's back.

'Are you sure this won't bring trouble on the village?' asked Pettic.

'No, these dagger fish travel miles. He'll be out of this moat and into the stream that feeds it in no time, especially now he's had a fright.'

The man slipped the fish, complete with dagger, into the water and watched him swim away.

'By the time they realize it's not you with the dagger, he'll be miles away. They'll have no idea where you attached it to him.'

Pettic grinned. 'Then I'd best be on my way. They said they'd come and get me. They know I made it to here, so the quicker I leave the better.'

The other man said, 'Come with me first. You need something to defend yourself with. There are bad things out there that'd like you for dinner, or breakfast, or just to kill you for fun.'

The pair of them went to the man's forge. He went to the back and picked up a sword. It was plain, but it had a good balance and was as sharp as it could possibly be made.

'Take this,' he said to Pettic. 'It'll help you defend yourself.'

Pettic thanked him and he and Cledo left Smithtown.

There were woods to the south of the village and Pettic made for them. He entered their depths and breathed a sigh of relief. He could not be seen from above, and there were plenty places to hide.

He peered out from a bush near the edge. When would the aerials come down to hunt for him? If what the smiths had said, it would not be long.

He walked carefully into the depths of the forest, trying to be as quiet as he could. He heard rustlings in the undergrowth and drew his sword. What was in these woods? He had already met three animals that he had not known about. How many more were there? How many were benign and how many were dangerous?

Then the next question entered his head. He had to get back to the city because he believed that was where the gem was. He also needed to be there in order to get back to Fusionem.

The only way was to go up with some aerials, and to do that he must be captured. Unless he could somehow disguise himself as an aerial. But how could he simulate the membrane?

He put the idea to one side for the moment and turned away from the village to walk into the forest to hide.

'I don't want him killed,' said Princess Eloraine, and she stamped her foot.

She was in the private quarters of her mother, the Queen. The queen paced the room, frowning, and her hands clenched and unclenched.

'We can't have groundlings wandering around the city willy-nilly,' she snapped.

She whirled to face her eldest daughter. 'They're to be sent to the ground. He's committed a crime coming here. He must pay for that crime.'

'Mother,' said Princess Sprinkla, taking her sister's side for once, 'we've no idea how he got to the city. We ought to bring him here to find out. If he managed it, then other groundlings might manage it too. We could be overrun. The Air alone knows there are enough of them.'

'Thank, you, Sprinkla,' said Eloraine, turning to her sister.

She turned back to her mother. 'What if they did find a way to get here? They could foment a revolution and wipe us all out. If they managed to get here and kill the magicians that man the artifacts keeping us in flight, then the Cities would all fall to the ground and everyone would be killed. No, they could easily wipe us all out unless we find a way to prevent them from getting here.'

'Are you forgetting we can fly?' The Queen turned to the girls. 'We could easily glide down to the ground just before we hit. Then we'd all be safe—at least most of us.'

Sprinkla sighed. 'True enough, mother, but if it were a revolution by the groundlings, then we'd be in great danger on the ground. There are, as I said before, an awful lot of them.'

The Queen sat down and narrowed her eyes.

'Why would the groundlings revolt? It's their nature to serve us. They're quite happy doing what they were created to do.'

'Well, I want him as a pet, whatever you say. I'm going to give the hunters instructions to bring him back alive.'

The Queen shook her head as she looked at her elder daughter. She sighed.

'I could over-rule your order, you know. The hunters would obey me rather than you.'

Eloraine smiled sweetly at her mother. 'But you won't, will you? You know I'll be queen after you and it's important the people get to see me as a dominant figure. So you won't undermine my authority.'

The queen raised her eyebrows. 'You're so sure of that?'

'Yes.'

Princess Eloraine and her sister turned and left the room leaving the queen unsure whether she was proud of or exasperated with her daughters.

Eloraine walked along the corridor to an open area. She stood looking out over the city, then she and Sprinkla jumped into the air and glided down towards the area from where Pettic and Cledo had been taken down to the ground. Once there, she walked over to a group of six people with brown hair and membranes.

'My sister and I are coming with you,' she told them. 'We're rather bored and want to go hunting. We don't want the groundling killed, either. We need to know how he got up into the city in the first place so he must be brought back here alive.'

The princesses went into a nearby hut and came out equipped with hunting bows. Once all were ready, the six hunters and two princesses leaped off the edge of the city and glided down to the ground. They landed close to a lake a few miles away from Smithtown.

'This was where the last signals came from, Your Highnesses,' said the chief hunter.

She was a tall woman and dwarfed all but one of the male hunters. She carried a bow and iron-tipped arrows as well as a nasty-looking spear. The other hunters, one more woman and four men, were similarly equipped, but one had a sword in a scabbard at his waist. This was for giving the final coup de grace if the groundling were not dead when they reached it.

The hunters searched round the lake for tracks. They found nothing.

'Are you sure the signals came from here?' asked Sprinkla.

'The magicians were certain. They said the signals followed the line of the river from the moat round Smithtown. It was last seen here.'

'Let's go to Smithtown,' said Eloraine. 'We'll perhaps be able to pick up the trail from there, or perhaps the smiths saw the direction it went in.

It was a long walk back to the village. They passed over several low hills and once at the top the aerials glided down the other side to rest their legs a bit. They were not used to walking long distances. By the time they saw the smoke from the many forges in the village they were very tired.

The smith Pettic first talked to saw them coming. He ran to the tavern to warn the others. Pettic's story swiftly travelled round the village and the villagers decided they would say nothing of the visit to the hunters. They felt sorry for him. Most believed his story and wanted him to succeed in his quest.

The smith ran back to his forge, and by the time the little band arrived he was hard at work.

'Ho, smith,' called the chief hunter. 'Have you seen a stranger around here? A groundling with a large grey animal with him.'

The smith gave a surly look. 'No, ma'am,' he said. 'I've been busy at my forge all day. No time to look for strangers, ma'am.'

Princess Eloraine stepped forward. The smith kept the same surly look on his face.

The princess spoke to him. 'Perhaps someone else in the village saw someone. Or perhaps something else unusual happened. Your boy goes out on errands, doesn't he? Perhaps he saw someone?'

The smith scowled even deeper.

'I told ye I saw no one. My boy would say if he saw someone. We've seen no one.'

One of the hunters stepped forward and slapped the smith hard across his face. In spite of his size, the smith staggered backwards.

'No need to speak to the princess like that. You groundlings need to understand just who you are. Nobodies.'

Eloraine looked at the smith, then she turned to the hunters. 'Give him a last reminder of his position in the world then we'll go and see if anyone else has noticed anything unusual.'

All the hunters converged on the hapless smith and his apprentice. One held the smith and another the boy while the rest began to beat them mercilessly.

After a few minutes, the princess, who watched with a slight smile on her face, said, 'Enough. I think they've learned how to speak to their betters. Animals have to be taught harsh lessons, don't they? A pity, but that's life.'

The group left the forge in search of someone else to ask.

After they had rounded the village and asked everyone, some getting beatings, others not, depending on how they answered, the hunters and princesses arrived back at the tavern. Here they demanded ale and also beds as darkness began to fall.

'But, Your Highnesses, Your Graces, we're only a tavern. We don't have beds.'

'Do you and your family sleep on the floor then?' asked Sprinkla, sweetly.

'N-no. We have beds. We all have beds,' stammered the tavern keeper,

'Then you'll let us have those beds, won't you?'

'But, Your Highness, where will we sleep? There's my wife and myself as well as our five children.'

'Six beds then. I can sleep with my sister in your bed. The others can decide how to arrange their sleeping. Where you and your family sleep is of no concern of ours.'

The poor tavern keeper and his family managed to get some sleep on the floor of the tavern, although the children were restless and the little one, a three year old boy, cried most of the night.

Next morning, before the sun was up, the hunting party came into the tavern room demanding breakfast. The tavern keeper's wife struggled to her feet and went out into the back to try to find something suitable for the visitors.

She came back in with a wheel of cheese and several loaves of bread. This she gave to the hunters and they ate every last scrap, washed down with more of the precious ale. The tavern keeper looked into his barrels. They were getting empty and there was no scheduled delivery from Brewertown for weeks yet. What would happen if he ran out? His regulars would be far from pleased. He only hoped they would understand.

Soon the 'guests' left and made their way to where the river left the moat after flowing round the town. The hunters searched along the river and after some distance they thought they could see some footprints, but they were unclear. There also seemed to be the prints of a wolf or similar animal amongst them. Was this evidence that Pettic had indeed come this way, or were the prints those of some of the villagers who had been here and the prints wolf prints.

They searched further on and found nothing more. The young man called Pettic seemed to have disappeared into thin air.

They walked on, following the river until they had nearly reached the lake where they gave up the previous day. As they gathered on its banks, Eloraine looked down into the water.

'What's that?' she asked.

'Only a dagger fish,' replied one of the hunters, turning his attention towards the trees at the bank.

'This one seems to have something on its back.'

They all looked to where Eloraine pointed. Sure enough, a dagger fish swam in the shallows with something clearly tied to it.

One of the hunters hefted his spear and threw accurately. The spear flew unerringly to its target, then the hunter reached in and pulled it out with the fish attached.

The princess looked at the dagger, for dagger it was, attached to the fish's body.

'This is the dagger we gave Pettic so we could track him. He's very clever for a groundling. We still don't know how he got to Smithtown so quickly.

'Indeed he is, your highness,' replied the chief hunter. 'It's almost as if he flew here. I'd not have expected anyone to be able to make that distance so quickly. He must have had help.'

'But where could he have got help?' queried Sprinkla 'None of the groundlings have the means of flying. Only the beasts.'

'One of the magicians said that, as he tracked the fugitive, he was moving very quickly and he thought it seemed almost as if he were flying, but that's not possible.'

They decided to leave that problem for another day and concentrate on the job in hand, which was finding where Pettic had gone.

.

Chapter 13

Pettic hid in the forest for a full day. While he was there, he looked around to find out more about where he was. Creatures lived there, but they disappeared at his approach.

Then he noticed a large nest in a tree. He approached it and found it had one large egg in it. This was not the season for birds to lay their eggs. His observations had indicated autumn rather than spring. He thought this one would likely not hatch, or if it did it would not survive through the winter.

He slipped back into the undergrowth when he spotted a beautiful bird flying down to the nest. It had feathers of blue, red and yellow with plumes of green coming from its head. It settled onto the nest to incubate its egg.

Suddenly, Pettic smelt burning. He looked up and saw smoke coming from the nest. The beautiful bird seemed not to notice. Pettic thought he must help. He climbed the tree expecting the bird to fly away, but instead she pecked at him. He took off his jacket and beat at the nest, which was now beginning to show flames. The mother bird showed no signs of flying away, and eventually Pettic had to climb down as the flames became too hot.

He felt sad such a beautiful creature should die and that its chick would not have a chance to live. He sat down below the tree and Cledo licked his face in sympathy.

Suddenly, he heard a beautiful song. He raised his head. The nest and bird were gone, but the egg was cracking. He stood up in wonder as from the ruins of the nest rose another beautiful bird, this time young.

After this wonder he sat and contemplated for some time. The old bird had sacrificed herself so her youngster could live. It obviously needed fire to hatch the egg and the older bird had spontaneously combusted to provide that fire.

When it started to get dark he crept back to look at the village again. Perhaps it would be safe to go back and trade for some food, although what he had to trade he had no idea.

Then he saw them. The aerials. They stood looking at the banks of the river. What were they looking for? Then it dawned on Pettic. They'd not been able to find him wherever the dagger fish had gone and so had come back to Smithtown to try to pick up his tracks from there.

As he watched he recognised Eloraine amongst the hunters. Why had she come down? The villagers had not given him any idea that some of the aristocracy might come down to hunt, although, come to think of it, hunting was mainly an aristocratic pursuit in his world.

The hunters moved further up the river and soon disappeared round a bend. Pettic took his chance and ran swiftly towards the village. He crossed the bridge and entered Main Street.

He heard sounds coming from the forge on his right, where he had first spoken to the smith on entering the village for the first time, but they were not sounds of smithing.

He entered the forge and saw the blacksmith lying on the floor with blood spattered about. His apprentice crawled towards him, moaning and crying. Pettic knelt by the lad.

'What happened here?' he said as he reached for a cloth and dipped it into a bucket of water. He listened to the mumbled words of the boy as he gently wiped the blood from his face.

The boy's face had swollen and his eyes were half closed and beginning to show black bruises. Pettic looked round. A bench stood at the back of the forge. He looked for some sacks to soften it a bit and then gently led the boy and laid him down on top of the sacks.

He then went to look at the still unconscious blacksmith. Pettic decided not to move him. He cleaned him up as best he could and went to the tavern to see if he could get some help.

Most villages in his world had a healer of some kind. Some were only herbalists, but others had some real healing skills. With all the trades being together in one village, he wondered if that were true of the healers. If so, he would have to go looking for another village. A village of healers. Still, that would not make any sense. To have a healer in each village would be more logical.

Once he reached the tavern, he entered and saw the tavern keeper and his wife peering into the barrels. He walked up to them.

'Is something wrong?' he asked.

'Something wrong? I'll say there's something wrong,' snapped the tavern keeper's wife. 'Those blasted aerials. Came in here last night, turned us out of our beds so they could sleep in them, including our little one, then drank nearly all our ale. We're not due another delivery for weeks. Nearly ruined us, they have.'

Pettic felt his anger rising. How dare these aerials treat these hard-working folk in this way? Beating the smith and his apprentice, then turning the tavern keeper and his family out of their beds–one of them only three years old.

He told them what had happened to the smith near the gate and they sent their daughter, an eleven year old, to the smith's house to tell his wife, and then to the old herbalist to go to tend to him.

The tavern keeper turned to Pettic when the arrangements had been made. 'They'll see to him and his apprentice now,' he said. 'Get someone to carry them home and see to their injuries.'

'You shouldn't let them treat you like this,' he told them. 'They treat you worse than animals.'

'What can we do?' said the tavern keeper, spreading his hands. 'We rely on them for our livelihood. Most of our goods go up to them.'

'You could try not sending the goods up. From the little I saw when I was up there, they've nothing there either to grow stuff or to make stuff.'

The tavern keeper's wife raised her brows. 'You might have an idea there,' she said. Then she looked crestfallen. 'But they'd send soldiers down and make us trade. We can't stand against all their soldiers and their weapons.'

Pettic thought for a few moments. It was true that the aerial soldiers could crush a simple village like this, but what if all the villages joined forces? There were far more villagers than city folk altogether, he estimated.

Then he had another thought. The way the aerials had been talking, there was more than one city. How many were there, he wondered.

He asked the tavern keeper's wife. She seemed to have taken charge since the tavern keeper himself was too upset about his ale, and she was just angry, especially at their little boy having to sleep on the floor.

'There are five,' she told him. 'Abrion, Kellor, Hrondir, Sellop and the one you came from, Faoor.'

'Why do they need weapons? They hunt, yes, but there seem to be too many smiths here producing weapons just for hunting.'

'Oh, the cities fight amongst themselves,' replied the wife. 'They all want to be the top city, you see. They're all independent with their own rulers, but that's not good enough. Each city wants to rule the others.'

'I see.'

Pettic walked away to the other end of the tavern to think. He sat down on a bench and absently petted Cledo, who revelled in the attention. Was there a way he could use this animosity of the cities for one another? Somehow he must help the groundlings gain some sort of freedom. They were slaves but did not actually realise it.

Eventually, Pettic had an idea. He went and put it to the tavern keeper. Their eleven year old daughter had just entered. She heard what was being said.

'Yes!' she exclaimed. 'I don't want to be taken away next year. I could be sent anywhere, or married to a horrid man. I want to stay here. Perhaps be a tavern-keeper and help Papa, or maybe a silversmith.'

'I'll talk to Natas, see what he thinks. He'll need to know anyway, and put it to the council.'

The wife turned to Pettic. 'Natas is the headman,' she explained.

Natas agreed to put Pettic's plan to the council. The smith was a well-liked man in the village and his beating had angered everyone. Anything that would help to get back at the aerials would have been welcome, but Pettic did not want to start a war between the aerials and the groundlings.

He sat down and worked out just how many aerials there were likely to be. The tavern keeper's wife told him all the cities were about the same size. That would mean that each of the five cities had a population, he estimated from what he had seen, of around 10,000. If one quarter were children, that left seven thousand five hundred adults.

Now, there seemed to be six different castes of aerials, red, brown, black, bronze, silver and gold. Only the blacks were guards and soldiers and so that meant that on each city, assuming an even split between the castes, of just under seven hundred fighters. That is assuming an equal split, which of course was not necessarily true. In his world, there were fewer of the aristocracy than the ordinary men and women. If this were the case here, there may be as many as one thousand five hundred soldiers in each city. Nine thousand soldiers altogether. Nine thousand trained fighters.

Pettic was not going to let it come to a fight, though. Not if he could help it, but he had to do something to help these people. He also felt, on some instinctive level, that it would help the aerials too.

As soon as night began to fall, Pettic fled the village and returned to the forest. He knew the aerials would return since they would not have found him. Just before dark, as he peered from the bushes, he saw the hunters returning. They were carrying something. Something long and thin. He peered but could not tell what it was from this distance.

The next day, as he saw the aerials leaving Smithtown, he crept slowly towards the village. He had to see if the villagers had agreed to his plan. Then he had to carry it out.

He arrived at the tavern and entered. The room was buzzing. Pettic raised his eyebrows as it was a bit early to be drinking, but then he noticed that no one had any ale in front of them. There were men and women and even some children there.

As he entered, a cheer rang out, quickly hushed by a tall, grey-haired man standing by the barrels.

'Quiet,' he said, 'The aerials won't have got far. We don't want them to hear and wonder what's going on.'

The company quickly quieted. The man, who turned out to be Natas, told Pettic the council agreed to his plan. It was about time the groundlings stood up for themselves.

Later that day, Pettic left the village. He was without his faithful companion, Cledo. He told the dog he was to stay with the tavern keeper until he returned. He had no idea if his plan would work. It relied on his relationship with the flying horse. Was she anywhere near? Would she respond if he called? He was about to find out.

He stood in the open land about half a mile from Smithtown. He whistled then turned round and whistled again. No response. Perhaps she and the foal had gone back to where he first encountered her.

He tried one more time, and was just going to return to Smithtown to tell them this thing was going to take longer than he thought when he saw a dot in the sky. The dot grew bigger and resolved itself into two dots. Eventually he recognised the mare and her foal.

They landed just before him and the mare knelt down to indicate he could mount. This he did and she took off. He guided her with his knees towards Brewerstown, a full thirty miles west of Smithtown.

As usual, they landed about half a mile from the town and he walked in. Like Smithtown, Brewertown was ringed with earthworks, but unlike Smithtown, no river filled the deep moat. Instead, that moat was full of sharpened stakes.

Pettic smelt the air. Yes indeed, this was Brewertown. He could smell the fermenting ale wafting towards him across the moat. The bridge was down and he crossed into the town.

Unlike Smithtown, Brewertown had the residences on the main street and the breweries behind, on side roads and near the walls. As he walked up the road, eyes watched him from the windows. He felt them on his back as he made his slow progress, looking out for someone to speak to.

Eventually he got to a square in the centre of the town. Here stood a building larger than the rest. It was not a brewery. It had windows down the sides and steps going up to double doors.

As he was trying to decide whether or not to enter, a man came puffing out of a side street.

'My wife came to tell me...' puff puff, 'that there's a stranger in town...' puff puff. The man put his hands on his knees and bent down to get his breath back.

'Oh dear,' he said. 'I'm not as young as I was, and nowhere near as young as you.' He took a deep breath and stood up.

Pettic looked at him. The man was in his early sixties and getting a little round in the middle. His hair was thinning and he wore spectacles. He now took them off, wiped them with a large piece of red cloth and replaced them.

He smiled at Pettic. 'Look, we don't get strangers here. Or anywhere on the ground, come to think of it. 'People just don't leave their towns. Only the delivery folk, and they're known by the people in the towns they visit. So you're not a delivery man. Who are you?'

Pettic looked down at the man, who was smaller than he was. 'My name's Pettic and I'm from another world.'

The man laughed. 'Yes, a good one that. Not heard that before.'

'It's true though. I come from a world called Fusionem. I take it you're the headman or some such. Is there somewhere we can talk.'

The man, who said his name was Harip, led Pettic into the large building.

'This is our council house. We hold council meetings here. People can come and watch if they wish. They sit over there.' He indicated a slightly raised area to the right of the doors. 'Come, let's go into the inner office. The chairs are more comfortable.'

Passing through a door at the far end of the hall, Pettic found himself in a room about one quarter the size of the large hall. There was a fireplace on one outside wall and Harip bent down and lit the fire that was laid there.

'Now, tell me all about yourself. No lies, mind.' He reached over to the mantle piece and lifted a pipe from a rack. Having filled it with tobacco, he tamped it down, then lit a spill from the fire and proceeded to light it. He indicated a chair to Pettic and sat down himself in another, crossing his legs and leaning back comfortably.

Pettic leaned forward.

'What I told you is the truth,' he said. He then related his story to Harip who listened with interest, interrupting every so often with a question.

When Pettic had finished, Harip looked at him hard. Pettic felt he was being stripped of all his skin and that Harip was seeing right into the truth of what he had told him.

'It's a strange story,' said Harip, 'but funnily enough, I believe you. No, not funnily at all. I asked you some questions that if you were lying you would have had at least to pause to think of a reply, but you didn't. You also didn't let me trip you up into contradicting yourself.'

Pettic thought this man was smarter than he looked. He replied, 'Thank you sir. Now will you hear me out? I've come from Smithtown on a very important mission.'

Harip stood up, knocked the ashes from his pipe into the fire and said, 'Just wait here for a bit, lad. I think everyone ought to know about this. I'll go and round up the rest of the council.' With that, he left Pettic sitting in the small room to wait.

It didn't take long for Harip to round up the other councillors. There were ten in all. As there were too many for the small room, they adjourned to the large hall. To Pettic's surprise, several of the villagers sat in the public area.

'People,' said Harip, when all were seated. 'This is Pettic. He's a very rare thing, a stranger. He says he's something of importance to discuss with us, from Smithtown.'

He turned to Pettic, 'First tell us your story.'

Harip sat, leaving the floor to Pettic. He looked around and then stood. He told his story to the assembled councillors and those of the public who managed to make it to the council house.

Pettic received a lot of skeptical looks as he took his seat again, but Harip once more stood and looked at the assembled people.

'I've talked to this young man and questioned him. I know his story sounds impossible, but I could find no flaws in it. I believe him. Now he says he has a message from Smithtown. I ask him to tell us what it is.'

Pettic stood again. He looked at the assembly and took a deep breath.

'I've just come from Smithtown as Harip told you. I arrived there, as I thought, to complete my punishment and be returned to Faoor to be the pet of Princess Eloraine, whatever that means. I discovered, though, that if any groundling manages to escape to a village, he or she is hunted by the aerials.'

He looked round the assembled people before continuing.

'I hid in the forest until the aerials went and then I went back to Smithtown. There I found the smith I first met had been badly beaten for not telling of my whereabouts. His apprentice too.'

Pettic pressed his lips together and his fingers clenched into fists

'I was very angry and when I found the aerials had turned the tavern keeper out of his bed, and all his family too, including his little three year old boy, I suggested they refuse to give their goods to the aerials.

'They, of course, said it was impossible. The aerials would come with their soldiers and subdue them.'

'Quite right,' called a voice from the back. 'That's exactly what would happen.'

Pettic looked towards the speaker.

'On Aeris, all one trade is gathered together into a separate village. This doesn't happen on other worlds. Each village or town has smiths, brewers, tanners, etc. They all live and work in the same place.'

There was a murmur at this strange idea, but it soon died down when Pettic raised his hand.

'This idea of keeping all of one trade in one place is a good one. You all rely on each other for what you need and so there's no fighting among the towns and villages. But it's also a weakness. If the smiths refuse to send the metal goods up to the Cities, then the aerials can't get them from anywhere else. The same for their ale, or their leather goods, or their food. You have power. You can starve them.'

Here he paused. Some people looked interested, but others looked skeptical, and a few looked afraid.

'From the little I saw while I was on Faoor, it seems they have no means of providing for themselves.'

There was uproar then. Some people seemed to think Pettic was mad and the aerials would attack in force and wipe out all the groundlings.

'How would they survive then,' asked another. 'They need us.'

The village council house slowly filled up as night approached and people finished their day's work. As it did, so the arguments increased. Soon, just before it became truly dark, Harip stood again.

'I think this needs a full village vote,' he said. 'In two days' time we will reassemble here. All those eligible to vote will be able to do so in answer to a question the council and I will set.

Two days later, Harip placed a board outside the council house. On it was written '*Do you think we should withhold our goods from the aerials in order to get better treatment?*'

All day, people walked up to the building, entered and picked up two balls from a table near the entrance, one white and one black. Then they walked to another table with a large pot standing on it. They dropped one of the balls into the pot. White for agreement, black for disagreement. They placed their unused ball in another pot then left. Pettic stood watching, hoping more white balls were going into the pot than black.

At the end of the day, the councillors took the pot into the small room at the back and counted the white and black balls.

They came out very quickly. This meant there was an overwhelming vote one way or the other. The councillors stood in a line and Harip stepped forward.

'People of Brewertown,' he began. 'Pettic here has spoken to us about withholding our goods from the aerials in protest of their treatment of us. They treat groundlings like animals and give us no rights. We are people and should not be treated in this way.'

'*Get on with it,*' thought Pettic.

'We have held a vote and now we will give you the result. Immoli, tell us what we have decided.'

A woman stepped forwards. She held a piece of paper in her hand, but did not look at it.

'I don't need to look at this.' She flapped the paper. 'The result was overwhelming with only half a dozen people disagreeing with the majority.'

Pettic was getting really anxious by now.

'The result is this. We have overwhelmingly agreed we should withhold our ale from the aerials.'

Pettic breathed a sigh of relief as cheering broke out in the hall. A few people with long faces left, but the majority remained to cheer and clap Pettic on the back.

The next day, Pettic left. He whistled and the flying mare returned. He repeated the procedure at all the villages he could find. Tanners, shoemakers, potters, hunters, miners, glassmakers, and many more all agreed to join the strike. Pettic did not visit the farmers, though, because they did not have the protection of a village and walls.

Finally, after a month of flying around, Pettic returned to Smithtown to report his success. The smith who had been beaten up had recovered, as had his apprentice, and everyone seemed anxious for the revolution to start.

They decided everyone must start at the same time and birds took messages to every village stating when they would begin. To allow for every bird to get through, Pettic suggested three months from now.

Chapter 14

'Where's he got to?' wondered Princess Eloraine.

'Stop worrying about your little groundling,' her sister snapped. 'I'm sick of hearing about him. Anyone would think you had a crush on him.

Eloraine looked at her sister, fury in her eyes.

'Don't be ridiculous. He's a groundling. Do you really think I'd be infatuated by an animal?'

'Peace, girls,' said Bramnor. 'Is he worth fighting over? A groundling?'

'No, not really,' replied Eloraine, 'it's just that I still can't make out how he got to Smithtown so quickly.'

'Maybe he flew!' smirked Sprinkla. 'Maybe he's an aerial after all and has a membrane that he can hide.'

'Shut up!' snapped Eloraine.

Just then their mother entered the room.

'Arguing again, girls?' she said. 'What's it about this time? Not that young boy from near the park? Although I can see why you might both be interested, He's very handsome.'

Both girls looked at their mother and answered together, 'No, certainly not.'

'Pity. Eloraine, you should be thinking of a mate, you know. You'll be queen one day and you'll need to ensure the succession. You need a daughter of your own.'

'They were arguing about that groundling,' Bramnor told her. 'You, know, the one that seems to have disappeared. Sprinkla was teasing Eloraine, saying she thinks El fancies him.'

The Queen looked shocked. 'I hope not, Eloraine,' she said. 'That would be the most terrible scandal and would probably bar you from the throne.'

'Don't be stupid, mother. I only wondered how he managed to get to Smithtown as quickly as he did.'

'We all wonder that, dear,' replied the Queen. 'Short of flying I really can't think of any other way.'

'Well, he can't have flown, can he?' said Bramnor. 'So that's that.'

Eloraine looked thoughtful.

'You know, there's another possibility,' she said. 'We tracked him through his dagger, didn't we? Suppose he found out somehow, perhaps from the farmer he stayed with, that we could track him through the dagger. Then caught the fish, strapped the dagger to it and released it somewhere near the farm. Those fish travel long distances and are known to be quite fast. Perhaps it was the fish we were tracking and not the groundling.'

'Hey, you might have something there, El.' Bramnor got to his feet and went and patted his sister on the back. 'That would explain how he got to Smithtown so quickly. He didn't, the fish did, so when you went to hunt him he wasn't there. He was still travelling. Perhaps he didn't get to Smithtown at all and the smith you had the hunters beat up was telling the truth after all.'

Eloraine waved her hand. 'That's immaterial,' she said. 'The hunters enjoyed it. Since we had no one to hunt they needed some fun somehow. And we didn't know he was telling the truth.'

'Anyway, children,' said the Queen, annoying her three offspring by calling them so, 'we've the ambassador from Kellor to eat with us and he's just arrived. We need to be nice to him if we're to make a treaty against Abrion. Don't be late. I've just heard he's landed, so come along and meet him.'

The four members of the Royal Family left the room to greet the ambassador.

The months passed quickly. The rebellion needed a lot of organisation. First, weapons were sent from one town to another. The smiths sent daggers and swords as well as spear and arrowheads.

In return they received food from some of the farmers who had decided they would help even if they could not actually take part.

The people from Arrowville made arrows and spears from the heads they received and sent them to every village and town. The bowyers in Bowham sent bows, the brewers sent ale to everyone. There was such a big transport of goods around it was a wonder the aerials did not see even from on high.

All the towns and villages stacked up supplies. Each one also began to train its citizens in the use of the weapons. They hoped they would not need to use them, but they had to know how, just in case.

Three months was not very long to learn, but all the citizens were motivated and practiced as much as they could. Even some of the children learned to use bows. The bowyers of Bowham made some smaller ones especially for the older children.

Then there came an influx of farmers. Many arrived in the towns because they felt the aerials would take revenge on them, but others came because they wanted to actively help and not feel useless.

One day, much to Pettic's delight, he saw Joert and Maoni along with their dog, approaching the town. He was pleased to see Maoni carrying the baby on her back. He had grown in the time since Pettic left them and appeared to be thriving.

The couple drove a cow in front of them and they tethered her on the grass before the town gates.

Pettic ran to the gate to greet the couple. They were as pleased to see him as he was to see them, but the two dogs growled at each other.

'Down, Cledo,' snapped Pettic, as the dogs started squaring up to each other. Both dogs reluctantly lay down, but still eyed each other.

'We may have to let them sort their differences out,' said Joert. 'One of them'll have to win or they'll never be able to live in the same town.'

Pettic reluctantly agreed, but until such a time, he stood to one side and let the couple through the gates.

Several of the townsfolk offered their homes to the farmers, some of whom had brought livestock with them, and others sacks of grain or other crops on wagons pulled by horses or oxen. This would all help if the aerials tried to lay a siege.

Soon everything was ready. Aerials had been to collect goods during the preparations, but the townsfolk managed to hide what they were doing. The aerials never entered the towns, all the collections were done outside. They thought the towns beneath their notice, and that they might contract some disease from what they had already decided were insanitary conditions. They had no reason for this assumption, but since groundlings were involved, and they were almost animals, it must be insanitary.

After three months of preparation, the sky overhead darkened. Pettic looked up. There, hovering above was one of the cities. He could not tell which city it was, but Natas, said that it was Hrondir they were expecting.

The first aerials descended to pick up their goods only to find the gates of Smithtown barred.

'Why are the gates closed?' demanded the leader of the delegation.

Pettic climbed to the top of the ramparts.

'We're not giving you any more goods until our demands are met,' he shouted.

'Demands?' the leader shouted back. 'You have no right to make demands. You're only groundlings.'

Pettic smiled. 'You're right. We have no rights. That's what this is all about. We demand the rights that any human being deserves.'

The aerial laughed. 'You aren't humans though, so you don't deserve, as you put it, 'rights'.'

'Think what you will,' Pettic called back. 'You're getting nothing until you negotiate.'

With that he jumped down from the earthworks and went back into the town.

The aerials hung around talking for a while, then they retreated to the pick-up point to the city. The ropes were lowered to pull them up and they left.

Some of the people began to cheer, seeing the aerials leaving, but Pettic and Natas quickly quieted them.

'This isn't the end,' Natas told them. 'They've just gone to report that we won't give them the goods. They'll be back to try to force us. This, people, is only the beginning.'

Two days passed. Hrondir hung overhead, cutting out the sun for much of the day. This put a dampner on the mood of the people, and Pettic and Natas did a lot of talking in order to keep spirits up.

Then, on the third day, the townsfolk saw several figures gliding down from the city. There were a dozen black soldiers and two gold high-ranking figures.

The figures landed and walked over to where the bridge usually crossed the moat. One of the soldiers called out.

'Hoy, Smithtown. We're here to give you warning. Listen to our Prince Ignormoran and take careful note of what he has to say.'

Pettic and Natas climbed up to the top of the wall. As soon as they appeared, one of the gold figures stepped forward.

'Hear me, citizens of Smithtown. You're in violation of your duty to the cities. It's your duty to supply us with whatever goods we require. If you do not do so, we will take the necessary steps to take the goods. That will not be pleasant and your ringleaders will suffer the greatest penalties. We'll return tomorrow in order to collect our orders. If they're not here, then prepare for trouble.'

Having said that, they turned round and left.

Pettic and Natas turned back to the town. A large crowd gathered in the streets near the gate. Natas spoke and told the citizens what the prince had said.

A man called out, 'We won't give in. Not now. We've come too far.'

A murmur of agreement came from everyone else. Pettic sighed. He thought perhaps in the face of reality some of the people might back down and want to give in, but no, all were still in accord.

That night, everyone met in the tavern. It was crowded and even the street outside was full. The whole population wanted to talk about what was about to happen the next day.

Much to the tavern keeper's chagrin, and Pettic and Natas's delight, few of the assembled citizens wanted to drink. They all wanted to have clear heads for the coming day, which they thought would surely bring fighting.

The next morning, soon after the town woke, the sentries on the wall called to say the aerials were arriving. There was Prince Ignormoran leading about fifty soldiers, all armed with long, wicked-looking swords. The party stopped before the gates and the prince called out.

'Hoy, Smithtown. We're here to collect our dues.'

There was no answer.

He called again.

Still no answer.

Then, a third time. This time he said, 'You're being given a last warning. Bring out our goods or take the consequences.'

Still no answer.

The prince then left the soldiers and went back to the ropes. He tied himself on and was hauled up.

Queen Kelle of Faoor read the letter that had arrived from Hrondir.

'I don't believe this,' she said, screwing up the letter in annoyance. 'How dare they?

'What are you talking about, mother?' asked Princess Eloraine. She took the letter from her mother and smoothed it out.

As she read it, her eyebrows rose.

'I see why you're angry,' she said, 'but you won't get anywhere by venting your anger on a letter. The people you should be angry with are the groundlings.'

'Send for the ambassadors of the other cities,' snapped the Queen. 'This must be discussed.'

An hour later, four ambassadors sat in the throne room of the palace on Faoor, waiting for the Queen to arrive.

They had all been in the throne room before, but it never failed to impress with the carved columns down each side and the dais with the beautifully carved and gilt throne standing on it.

The windows that ran down each side had stained glass scenes of historical happenings on Faoor and on the ceiling was a fresco showing the five cities flying above Aeris.

The ambassadors did not have long to wait. Queen Kelle entered with her eldest daughter, Princess Eloraine. The pair made their way through the bowing ambassadors to the throne where the Queen took her seat and the princess sat in a smaller, but no less elaborate chair to the Queen's right.

The ambassadors sat at a gesture from the Queen. She looked at each of them in turn and began to speak.

'I received a letter from the King of Hrondir this morning. There's a problem with the groundlings. They're refusing to send us the goods we ordered.'

She paused as the ambassadors gasped and began to murmur among themselves.

'It seems to me that we must teach them their place in the scheme of things. None of the cities has enough soldiers to do this alone. We must bury our differences, at least for the time being, and tackle this together.'

There was a murmur of agreement.

'I think we need to do two things. First, we must lay siege to each of the towns. This will stop them from getting food and any goods they may need. They'll give up when they get hungry and start dying.

'Second, we must find out who is behind this. It's very strange that this has happened all of a sudden when there has never been any sign of it before.'

The Queen stood and walked down the steps to where the four ambassadors sat. She looked each one in the eye before continuing.

'I command you all to send birds to your cities and tell them of this. Then we can plan and co-ordinate our descent to the ground.'

The Queen turned and, followed by Eloraine, left the ambassadors in a state of shock. They quickly recovered and, after a few minutes discussion of the information the Queen had just given them, each one left for his or her residence to comply with the Queen's wishes.

It took several days for the messages to get to the different cities and the replies to get back to Faoor, but every one expressed horror and agreed they must act in unison.

The messages from the other cities told of rebellion in the other towns. It was not just Smithtown that was refusing to send up goods, but every single town on the ground. Even the farms joined. They were abandoned and the stock and crops left to fend for themselves.

This was serious. The cities did not produce anything and if there were no food, then they would starve. They were, to all intents and purposes, under seige themselves. This must be resolved as soon as possible. Although the farms were unguarded, the aerials could not gather the food themselves as they had no skills in killing and butchering animals, or harvesting crops, milling flour and the many other things done by groundlings.

Princess Eloraine had been thinking. There had never been any unrest by the groundlings before. What was different now? The only thing she could think of was Pettic.

They assumed the stranger was dead, but suppose he was not? Could he have something to do with this? She wrinkled her brow as she sat in the window of her room thinking.

Perhaps Pettic had got to Smithtown after they had left. When he saw what they had done in beating the smith, perhaps he decided something must be done.

He claimed to have come from another world. Suppose he really had? If his world were organised very differently from Aeris, perhaps what they took as natural, was not so on his world. Perhaps there were no creatures who were, like the groundlings, barely human. If so, he would not be able to understand that fact.

These thoughts were very difficult for Eloraine to contemplate and she closed her eyes and sighed. She picked up a book to try to take her mind off such disquieting thoughts, but the thoughts would not go away.

Chapter 15

Birds arrived from the other towns to Smithtown. It seemed that Hrondir had sent messages to all the cities, and they agreed to put aside their differences and join their armies together to teach the groundlings a lesson.

Shortly afterwards, a huge black cloud floated down from the city hovering above. It quickly resolved itself into hundreds of soldiers with a few bronze leaders. They landed and made their way towards Smithtown where they spread themselves around the town. The siege had begun.

For the first few hours, not much happened. The soldiers patrolled round the earthworks and occasionally one of the bronze commanders walked past the gates. They seemed to be looking to see if they could find a way into the town, but they did not succeed. If they had true flight they could fly over the walls, but they did not, so they were limited to walking round and round.

The townspeople, and the farmers who came to take refuge, watched to see what would happen next. Not much, it seemed. The aerial soldiers continued to walk round and round until eventually they stopped and formed groups.

Pettic watched with interest to see what they might do. Eventually, they erected tents in neat rows and lit campfires. They had some groundlings with them. These slaves began to cook food for the soldiers, who settled down to eat.

Pettic frowned as he saw the aerials throw food in the direction of the groundlings, just as if they were dogs. How could people treat others in this way?

He turned away eyes blazing. These aerials thought they had a right to treat the groundlings in just any way they wanted. It would serve them right if the same thing happened to them.

A couple of days passed and still nothing happened. Boredom began to set in inside Smithtown. The smiths were still making their wares, mainly weapons, but they could not send the arrowheads to Arrowville nor receive arrows back. As they had not actually used any yet, they still had a full complement. That was not a problem.

Then one day the aerials sent their slave groundlings to cut down some trees. The people of Smithtown watched from their earthworks, brows furrowed. What were the aerials going to do with trees?

As they watched, it became clear to Pettic what was happening. They were building structures. Tall, wooden structures.

Pettic called to Natas who was about a hundred yards further down the embankment.

'Hey, I know what they're doing.'

Natas came running up.

'What?' he asked.

'They're building towers so they can launch themselves over our defences. We should try to destroy them before they manage to finish. Get rags and soak them in oil. We can light them and burn the towers.'

This kept the townspeople and farmers busy. They brought out all their old clothes and the children tore them up into pieces. Then they soaked them in the vats of oil that some of the men heaved over to the square. Women tied the oil-drenched rags to arrowheads and gave them to other children who ran to the ramparts with them.

Pettic and Natas organised the archers. They were not much as archers They had not had a great deal of practice, but they could mainly shoot straight and many of them would be able to shoot well enough to pick out a large target.

Boys came round with torches, each boy stopping by one group of archers. Every archer lit an arrow and, at the command from their leader, let fly. Many arrows missed, some hitting the builders, which they all regretted, but enough hit the wooden towers to set them alight.

A cheer rose from those who could see what was happening and the message soon reached those congregating in the town square and cheering erupted.

'Well, that's taught them,' said one old smith as he lowered his bow.

'Don't be so sure,' Pettic told him. 'These aerials are clever. As clever as we are, even if they don't use their brains much that I can see. They'll come up with something else.'

Sure enough, the aerials did not give up. They sent their slaves to chop down more trees and began to build more towers, but this time out of arrow shot. When this news got through to the townspeople, they groaned.

'They'll need to bring them nearer, though, won't they? They can't glide into town from that far away,' said a boy who was listening to his parents' conversation.

'Well, I suppose that's true,' said his father, looking at him and scratching his head. 'We can destroy them when they move them then.'

That was not to happen. The aerials built the towers much higher than the originals. Even so, the people of Smithtown were dubious as to whether the aerials could get enough height to glide over the earthworks and moat.

To their surprise, the aerials did not move the towers. As they watched from the earthworks, Pettic and Natas saw the aerials lighting fires between where they had built the towers and the walls of Smithtown. Natas turned to Pettic, a frown on his face.

'What are they doing?' he asked the young man. Pettic ignored him and turned to the messenger boy who was sitting stroking Cledo.

'Go and tell all the archers to come to the walls immediately. Oh, and take Cledo with you. I don't want him hit by a stray arrow.'

'But what are they doing?' reiterated Natas.

Pettic turned to him.

'Building thermals,' he said as he raised his bow in readiness.

Sure enough, as soon as they lit all the fires and they were burning well, aerials climbed the towers. They launched themselves from the top. As they glided, they steered themselves towards the fires and as they passed over them the rising hot air gave them lift. In this way they gained enough altitude to get over the earthworks and moat.

Natas had gone to the other side of the town leaving Pettic in charge of the gate side. The young man looked at his archers and checked the piles of arrows at their feet. The boy had come back from his errand and stood ready to run for more arrows if it looked as though they would run out.

'Nock an arrow,' called Pettic. 'On my call, let fly, but not before.'

The aerials were getting closer but were still not in range. One over-anxious man released his arrow and it fell far short.

'I said, wait until I give the order,' shouted Pettic towards him.' That's one arrow we don't have any more.'

The men and women on the earthworks held their nerve. They all longed to release their arrows. It seemed the aerials were getting too close. Surely they would be over the ramparts any minute.

'Take aim,' called Pettic, 'Now loose.' A cloud of arrows flew into the air.

Many missed their target, inexperienced as the shooters were, but some got through and hit aerials. None of the aerials were killed, but a couple had their membranes torn and plummeted to the ground, one landing in the moat where she flapped about until she disappeared under the water and did not resurface.

'Now, fire at will,' shouted Pettic and arrows flew through the air. Some of the aerials landed short and began to run back to their camp, but some made it over the ramparts. They landed in the streets of the town.

Men and women with swords patrolled those streets. The aerials drew their own and grouped together to move in. They, however, did not know the town and the townsfolk did. Sometimes they were attacked from behind, sometimes people ran in front of them and they charged after them only to find their prey had vanished.

One aerial ran into a child who had somehow got separated from his parents. The aerial raised her sword but Cledo, trotting down a side street looking for Pettic, saw what was about to happen and leaped at the woman. He grabbed her arm just before it came down and, growling, he worried it like he worried his toys at home. Her membrane tore and she screamed. A townsman heard that scream, came up behind and brought his smith's hammer down on her head. Her scream was cut off short. The smith, recognising the child, picked him up and, patting Cledo on the head and praising him, carried the child back to his home.

Soon every aerial who had got into the town was dead and the attack from the towers stopped. The townsfolk patted Natas and Pettic on the back and carried them, shoulder high, to the town square.

Natas stood on the steps leading to the town hall's main doors.

'Well, that's one battle won, I think, but I don't suppose it'll be the last. Go and get yourselves some rest and be ready for another one tomorrow.' He stepped down and walked over to Pettic.

'How long do you think this will go on?' he asked.

'I really don't know,' said Pettic. 'We can hold out until our food's all gone, but what then? The aerials, too, have a food problem. I suppose they have some stored in the cities, but how much can the cities spare for the troops on the ground? Everyone will start to get hungry and I think it just depends on who has the most food stored.'

Natas looked at the ground. 'I suppose we ought to ration what we have. That won't be very popular'

'No, but essential. I expect the people will understand.'

Natas then sent a cryer round the town asking all citizens to bring out what food they had. They could keep one day's food in their houses but all other food must be brought to the square to be stored. A ration for each household would be given out every morning.

People began to bring their food immediately. Most saw the value in what was being done, but, of course, there were a few who brought it reluctantly and even a few who tried to hoard some. This was unsuccessful in the main because their neighbours gave them away.

That evening, people ate the last of the food in their homes and went to bed expecting to be hungrier in the following days.

All evening and well into the night, Pettic and Natas catalogued the food and decided just how much each person required. Small children and babies would not be allowed to go hungry, but everyone else would be expected to pull in their belts.

There were, surprisingly, few grumbles at the amount of food given out the next morning. Wives took what they had been given and used their ingenuity to prepare appetising meals, but even so, people went to their stations on the battlements not feeling as full as on previous days.

Pettic saw several of the aerial commanders going into one tent and deduced they were holding a meeting. Then one came out and went to where the city had hovered to let them come down. He took a device and did something, but Pettic could not see what, nor make out what the device was. He could see it had a gem in it, so it was probably a magical device.

The commander did not have to wait long, perhaps half an hour at most, when a city appeared overhead. He held onto the ropes they dropped and was hauled up.

'*Now what's going on there?*' he wondered.

The commander, whose name was Varen, went immediately to the royal palace. He asked for an audience with the Queen. It was indeed Faoor where he had arrived. He was admitted immediately into the Queen's private quarters.

He bowed as he entered, and the Queen beckoned him forwards.

'You have a report for me, I think,' she said.

'Yes, your Majesty,' Varen replied. 'We attacked the smiths yesterday. We thought if we got the slaves to build towers we could glide over the walls and take the town.'

'A good idea. How did it work?'

'The first towers the smiths burned with fire arrows so we built more out of arrow range. Then we built fires to create thermals so we could get over the walls from a greater distance.'

Haren shuffled his feet and looked at the ground.

The Queen watched him carefully noticing his discomfiture.

'How did this attack go wrong then?' she asked.

Haren raised his eyes and met hers.

'The groundlings had lots of bows and arrows. They fired them at us and prevented many of us from getting as far as the walls. We only lost one soldier, though. The smiths aren't very good archers, but there are quite a number of wounded, some with slashed membranes who won't be able to fly for a few weeks.'

'Did any of you get over?'

'Yes, quite a lot, actually.'

'And?'

'We don't know. They never came back.'

Queen Kelle stood, her lips compressed into a thin line and her hands clenched into fists at her sides.

'Go back and tell your colleagues that you need to do better. Somehow you need to neutralise those arrows. Without them you should be able to get in.'

Varen bowed but did not move.

'Is there something else?'

'Yes, Your Majesty. The groundlings are besieged in their towns. They won't be able to get food or more weapons. That's good, but what isn't so good is that we, too, are going to run out of food. We need more supplies.'

The Queen frowned.

'That could be a problem, you know,' she said. 'We have only a limited amount in the city, and the same will go for the other cities too. I suggest you try to get this battle won as quickly as you can and then food shortages won't be an issue.'

She turned and left Varen looking after her, bemused by her refusal to allow them more food.

A similar thing was happening on the other cities. All the besieging armies realised they were going to get hungry. Some of them reported failed attacks while others had been unable to figure a way of succeeding in an attack.

All the rulers of the cities had to think of their citizens. Their argument to themselves was that if they let those at home go hungry, then there might be a riot that would put them in danger.

The next day, Varen returned with the Queen's message. All the commanders were angry.

'If we don't win here,' said the Commander in Chief, 'then it's the end of the aerials. We can't live without the groundlings.'

'Does she realise that?' asked the commander of the west flank.

'She should. If she doesn't then she's got no right to be queen,' said the commander of the north flank

'Careful! That sounds like treason,' said the commander in chief.

'Well, she's an intelligent woman and so ought to see the importance of us here on the ground. We're more important than those people up there who sit around doing nothing except playing all day.'

The argument went on, but the lack of food was not resolved.

Up in the city, the Queen talked to Eloraine.

'Mother, they need food down there' said the princess. 'If they don't win, what will become of us?'

'And, Eloraine,' retorted the Queen, 'what will become of us if the people riot and depose us as reigning monarchs. That has already happened in history, you know. Our house only rules here because your great, great, great grandpa rebelled against the then Queen and put his wife on the throne.'

'If we don't send them food, mother, then they won't have the strength to win against the groundlings. There are so many more groundlings than aerials. Why not send some hunters down? They can catch food for the troops and fight the groundlings from a distance with their arrows.'

The Queen reluctantly agreed and sent out an edict rationing the food in the city. She then sent down some of the hunters with food and a good supply of arrows for the soldiers.

They were greeted with a loud cheer which made the watchers on the earthworks wonder what was happening.

Chapter 16

There was a shape in the sky. It grew bigger, then resolved itself into three shapes. As they neared, Pettic wondered what they were. At first he thought perhaps the pegasus mare was returning, but it soon became obvious that these things were not pegasi.

As they approached, the smith who was standing next to Pettic on lookout, exclaimed, 'That one in the front is a sphinx and the other two are griffins. What are they doing here?'

The creatures circled the town and landed in the square. People ran to see what was going on, including Pettic.

The sphinx folded her wings and settled down in the middle of the square.

'Where is the young man who helped the pegasus?' she demanded in a booming voice.

'I'm here,' said Pettic, panting as he ran into the square.

The sphinx looked at him. 'Hmm,' she said, and tossed her head. 'You don't look like much. Why did you help the pegasus?'

Pettic looked at the creatures. The sphinx was huge. Her body was similar to that of a lion with the head of a beautiful woman. She had wings like those of an eagle folded along her back.

The other two creatures, griffins, also appeared to be mixtures of animals. They had the forequarters of an eagle and the hindquarters of a lion. They remained standing and looking round the square at the people gathered there, as if waiting for an attack. Pettic surmised these were bodyguards for the sphinx, although why she would need them, he was unsure. She looked more than capable of defending herself.

He decided he had better tell the truth.

'I saw she was getting the worst of the fight. She was so beautiful that I didn't want her to die.'

'The wyvern, however, was fighting to get food for his offspring. You wounded him and his youngsters went hungry that day and the next two.'

Pettic hung his head. 'I'm sorry for that, but the pegasus's foal was saved. It would have died if its mother had been defeated.'

'Yes, it would, but that is the nature of things. Then in the forest you nearly prevented the birth of a new phoenix by trying to put out the fire that is essential for its birth.'

Oh dear. This was going badly. Pettic felt on trial. Perhaps he was. He looked the sphinx in the eyes.

'I did that because I thought both the mother and the chick in the egg would die in the fire. I didn't know it was essential for the chick to go through fire and the mother to die. I'm sorry I nearly prevented the birth of such a beautiful creature.'

'So, you only think about beauty? Is that your only criterion for saving something?'

Pettic stuttered. 'Well…I…I…I don't think so. I hope not. I believe all things have a right to life.' Here he paused and thought. 'I suppose that means some things dying in order that others might live. Wolves, in my world, kill deer to survive, and even humans kill other creatures to live.'

'You're getting the idea now,' the sphinx said. 'I believe you acted in innocence in both cases. Your intentions were good. I will therefore get my creatures to help you. They will carry things you need to fight these aerials. The aerials hunt the creatures here for fun and not for food alone. That is not good.'

She looked round the square and seemed to weigh up the people standing there.

'We visited them before coming to see you,' she continued. 'They shot at us and so we will not help them, although we want peace to return to Aeris.'

Pettic bowed to the huge creature before him. It was obvious that she was somehow the queen of the beasts on Aeris.

'All we want, Your Magnificence, is for the groundlings to be treated in a decent and respectful way, and not as slaves.'

As she stood, she turned back to the people and looked around again.

'Yes, the way you folk have been treated is wrong. I wish you success. With our help you may yet win. We will move all the animals that the aerials might hunt away from the areas where they are camped. That will help you as well. I think. We will now visit the other sites of siege and tell them what we have decided here.'

With that comment. she and the two griffins leaped into the air with a tremendous downbeat of their wings. It caught some people unawares and they staggered under the draught. When they recovered, the creatures were again three specks in the sky.

The very next day three wyverns flew over and dropped some packages. Natas was passing through the square and he ran and picked them up. They were parcels of food. Some meat and some vegetables. He ran to Pettic with the news.

'Well, they're doing as they said,' Pettic mused. 'I wonder if we can get messages to other towns this way? It would be useful to be able to send arrowheads to Arrowville and get arrows back in return. Those we have won't last if the siege goes on too long.'

'Just a thought,' Natas said, 'but we're lucky here in that we've plenty of water. After all, the moat is inside the earthworks. Some towns have wells, but there are one or two that have to go out of the town to a river or stream. They'll run out of water. Do you think we could send water to them?'

Pettic thought. The pegasus he had begun to think of as 'his' came when he whistled. He stood on the embankment, put his fingers in his mouth and a shrill sound emerged.

He waited for a while, then repeated the whistle. Cledo looked at him. Pettic patted the dog.

'I know you're there, boy,' he told the dog, 'but I'm whistling for a pegasus, not you.'

After a few minutes, a pegasus flew into the town and landed in the square. Pettic went up to it. It was not the one he had saved and ridden. It was a stallion. The creature bowed to him and waited. Pettic bowed in return and asked the creature if it would carry water to the mining community in the mountains. The stallion bowed his head in acquiescence and allowed the townspeople to load barrels of water on his back.

The pegasus took off in the direction of the mountains and Pettic looked at Natas.

'Well, we seem to have that problem sorted out,' he said to the other man as the people cheered.

Then there came a cry from the earthworks to the east. Pettic and Natas rushed to see what was happening.

When they got there, they had to duck the arrows coming towards them. The aerial commanders had got the hunters to shoot at the people manning the walls.

They commanded everyone to jump down behind the barrier. Already a few bodies lay on the top of the earthworks.

This was a new development. Up until this time, the towns-folk had the advantage of being able to shoot from a distance, but now the aerials had that too. One thing Pettic realised, though, was that they could get more arrows but the aerials could not.

Sure enough, the aerials stopped firing as soon as they could see no one to fire at.

Pettic thought. They ought to erect something they could fire through or around but that would prevent the aerials from hitting the archers who were firing. The idea was good, but how to erect something without coming under fire themselves.

Eventually, he and Natas decided they would need to erect a barrier at night. They began by collecting all the wood, boxes, large pieces of metal and anything else that could be stacked. People brought all kinds of things to the square. Being a town full of smiths, all iron was taken and melted down, then reforged into sheets. The smiths cut narrow holes in the sheets, wide enough to see to fire an arrow through. They then melted the metal they had cut out to make more sheets.

There was not quite enough to make a complete ring around the town's earthworks, but the most vulnerable places could be covered.

It took couple of days before they had all the sheets ready. Pettic and Natas organised groups of men to dig trenches in the earthworks at night. Then, others carried the sheets up and partly buried them in the ground.

Archers crouched down behind the sheets and looked through the arrow slits. They had a good view of in front, but not so good to the side. However, there were sufficient slits so that it was not a problem. They would be covered by the archers on each side.

The next day, archers sat behind the barrier waiting for the assault. At first they heard the ping of arrows bouncing off the metal sheets, but they quickly stopped as the aerials realised they could not get their arrows through the slits as easily as the defenders could shoot at them. They lost a dozen of their number before they stopped.

They managed to get a few arrows through, and two of the defending archers were injured, but apart from that, the barrier was a great success.

A couple more days passed. The aerials decided to try to glide over the defences again. This time they sent the hunters first. As they flew over, the archers of the town picked them off as before, but when they were over the barrier, they folded their membranes and as they fell they shot arrows into the men and women behind it.

Many fell, either injured or dead. Many of the attackers also fell, but a lot got into the town. There were not only hunters, but soldiers too. Fighting began in the streets again. This time, having archers with them, the aerials could also attack from afar.

One part of the town was overrun. The citizens from that area ran into the square. There was panic. More aerials flew over the barrier and it looked as if the town was going to be overrun. Pettic was distraught. What he thought to be a great defense was turning out to be the means the aerials used to get into the town.

Then he had a thought. He whistled twice and a wyvern appeared. It landed in the square. Pettic spoke to it, hoping it understood him, and asked it if it would go for help.

The creature took off and headed westwards. Fighting continued in the streets of Smithtown. Some of the smiths fought with their hammers, preferring to use a familiar implement rather than a sword, which they had not had time to become used to using, let alone become proficient in.

The battle was bloody. Night drew in. Pettic and Cledo fought two black aerials in a back street. The aerials were surprised to find someone who knew how to use a sword in this town and consequently were getting the worse of it. Cledo hung onto the sword arm of one of the soldiers and Pettic, after dispatching the one he was fighting, quickly took the sword out of her hand.

She tried to run, but Pettic grabbed the membrane and it tore. She sank to the ground and sobbed.

'Right,' said Pettic. 'Come with me.'

He took his prisoner to the town hall where he found about half a dozen other prisoners. Natas took them and locked them up in a cell.

The battle stopped with nightfall, although one section of the town was still occupied. The people from that area were accommodated in the homes of other citizens.

Pettic and Natas went to the town hall early the next morning. They entered the cell where the aerial prisoners were being kept.

'We want to talk to your commanders,' said Natas.

'Are you going to give up then?' asked one of them. 'You'll soon run out of food and arrows, then you'll have to give up or die.'

Natas laughed. 'You need food as much as we do. Where's yours coming from?'

The man smiled. 'We have our hunters. They can catch our food. You can't even leave your town to get some.'

'How much have your hunters caught in the last few days?' Pettic asked.

'Not much in the last couple of days,' replied the man, 'but that's how hunting goes, so the hunters say.'

'What if I tell you this will continue. You won't find any game in these woods. We have allies that have seen to it.'

'The beasts we've seen flying over here?' exclaimed the woman Pettic had brought in. 'They're helping you, aren't they?'

Pettic nodded.

She turned to her companion who had just been speaking. 'We must tell the commander this. It makes all the difference.'

'We'll let one of you go to speak to your commander. Tell him we want to talk,' Natas said to her.

The man who had spoken, who was obviously one of the leaders, answered.

'I'll go and tell our commander-in-chief what you want. Do I get to tell him what your demands for surrender are?'

'Who said anything about surrender?' Natas's eyes blazed. 'We have no intention of surrendering, but would be willing to come to a peaceful conclusion. We don't want any more people on either side to die.'

They agreed the prisoner should be released to go and talk to the commander in chief. Four armed smiths escorted him to the gate, the gate opened a crack and he left.

'Now we wait,' said Pettic as he sat down on the ground by the gate.

Before long, a bronze aerial walked towards them flanked by four others. Two were black ones and two were brown ones. The brown ones had arrows nocked to their bows.

Natas climbed to the earthworks and from behind the barrier he shouted, 'Only the commander. No soldiers or hunters. We will attack if they come any further.'

The commander said something to the four with him and they stopped. He walked slowly to the gate alone.

As it opened a crack, Pettic stood up and beckoned the commander through. Natas came down from the earthworks to meet the other two behind the gate.

'I am Natas, headman of this town. I would like to stop this bloodshed.'

'And why should we do that? You're here to serve us and you're refusing to do that. You deserve your punishment. Many of you will die unless you resume your delivery of the goods you owe us.'

'Perhaps. But how many of you will die too? There are fewer of you and most aren't soldiers. And the food supply will dry up. You're in as much a siege as we are. There's little game left in these woods and a limited supply of food in the cities.'

'The farms are left unattended. We can get food from there.'

'Can you milk cows then and turn the cream into butter? Can you cut the grain and winnow it, then grind it into flour? Can you make the bread from that flour? Can you kill and butcher an animal? And what about other things? Can you shear a sheep and spin the wool? Can you weave it into cloth and make that into clothes? Can you tan leather and...'

'All right,' snapped the commander. 'You've made your point.'

'I think you need these people more than they need you,' put in Pettic. 'If I were you I'd go back to my Queen or King and suggest you hold talks.'

'Is that it?' said the commander. 'Is that all you wanted to say?'

'Yes,' said Natas. 'That's it. I suggest you call off your attacks and your people surrounding this town and do as my friend Pettic says.'

The commander in chief whirled round and left.

'Don't think he was very impressed, do you?' Natas asked Pettic.

Pettic laughed. 'No, but when our allies arrive, perhaps he'll change his mind.'

'You're sure they'll come?'

'Pretty sure, yes.'

The battle started again the next day. The aerials had built large catapults and began flinging rocks over the barrier. Some of the barriers were hit and damaged. Several of the groundling archers were killed and a few others wounded. Those who could continue insisted on staying on the walls and fighting.

Another wave of aerials flew over while the defenders tried to set light to the catapults.

More died.

Then, all of a sudden a dark cloud appeared on the horizon. It got bigger as it approached. Soon it resolved itself into dozens of flying creatures. As soon as they were close enough, they began to attack the flying aerials.

There were pegasi, who landed in the town and cantered up and down the streets fighting the invading aerials with hoof and teeth. There were wyverns and griffins who attacked the flying aerials. There were winged snakes like the one Pettic had killed and they went into the camp of the aerials along with phoenixes and cocatrices.

The defenders looked on with amazement as the creatures decimated their enemy.

The commander in chief must have managed to send a message to Faoor because in the middle of this slaughter the city arrived overhead and the surviving aerials ran to the ropes where the people in the city pulled them up.

As soon as the last of the aerials had gone, the creatures flew away, but one was arriving. She flew in and landed in the town square as she had before.

She settled down on her haunches and called for Pettic.

He came hurrying from the walls and bowed to her. 'Thank you for the help of your creatures,' he said.

'I hope you will be able to negotiate now that they have left. My creatures have also taken care of the other towns. All the aerials have now gone. It is up to you now to make peace.' She stood up. 'I hope you will be able to free these folk from their slavery.'

With that she spread her wings. Pettic and Natas, having experienced the back draught previously, braced themselves as she leaped into the air and was gone.

Natas and Pettic looked at each other.

'We need to get a message up to the cities,' said Natas.

'Yes. I'm not sure how we do that though.'

They did not need to worry over that, though. The next day a red aerial came to the gates.

'I am here with a message from Queen Kelle. She wishes your leaders to come up to Faoor tomorrow one hour after dawn. Her Majesty wishes to speak with you. The leaders of all the towns are being invited to the cities.'

Then the aerial turned and left.

'Well now, what do you make of that?' said Natas.

'Could be a trap,' replied Pettic. 'I suggest we're very careful, but we must go.'

'*And I need to find that gem and get out of here,*' he added to himself.

Chapter 17

'Eloraine, you ought to come to this meeting,' her mother said the next morning. 'It'll be valuable experience for you. Negotiating is always tricky.'

'Do you really intend to negotiate, Mother?'

'Of course, dear. That groundling, what's his name, Naras, Natas? Anyway, he had a good point. Without the groundlings, we aerials are dead. We have to negotiate.'

Eloraine sighed. 'All right, I'll be there.'

The throne room had a large table in the middle. The slaves brought it here for the negotiations. Around it sat Queen Kelle, Princess Eloraine, Tromb, the aerials' first minister, Pettic, Natas and Harip from Brewerstown.

Queen Kelle began the proceedings.

'Now, we're here to try to come to some agreement,' she said. 'We need each other, it seems and fighting is not going to get us anywhere.'

'*The groundlings could get on quite well without you lot,*' thought Pettic, but he said nothing. He was concentrating on a slight warmth in his left earring indicating that the gem he was looking for might be close by.

The negotiations began. Queen Kelle spoke.

'First, what are your grievances?

'Where to start, Your Majesty,' Natas began. 'First, there is the treatment of us. Although we're not slaves in name, in practice that's exactly what we are.'

'What nonsense,' snapped the Queen. 'You're free to go where you will on the ground and you govern yourselves.'

'But we're not free to choose our own trades. Our children are taken from us as soon as they reach twelve years old and are put into whatever trade you decide is best for them.'

'You groundlings aren't capable of deciding what's best for you. You need guidance.'

Pettic's eyes narrowed and he clenched his fists beneath the table.

'With all due respect Your Majesty,' he said, through gritted teeth, 'the groundlings are intelligent beings. They are not something less than you.'

'The way of Aeris is that we aerials are the rulers and you groundlings are the ruled. We know better than you what is best for you.'

Pettic was unable to keep his anger in check any longer and he banged his fist on the table.

'You are not so different from the groundlings. I know that sometimes aerials give birth to a child without a membrane. Doesn't that suggest you are the same?'

'Those children are defective. We send them down to the ground where they'll be happier.'

'You send them down to die,' said Harip. 'A few we find, but too often we find small skeletons. It's inhumane.'

'You don't seem to have aerial children though,' Eloraine said. 'Doesn't that imply we aren't the same. If we were, you would have aerial children in the same way we have groundling children.'

'Oh, but we do,' said Harip through gritted teeth.

'How is that? You don't send any up to the cities.'

'When a baby is born with a membrane, we surgically remove it, Your Highness.'

The Queen's eyes flashed. 'You do what?' she exclaimed. 'You deny your children the right to live a comfortable life in the cities and instead condemn them to a life of hard work and drudgery?'

'There's nothing wrong with hard work. It's better than idleness,' retorted Natas. 'And what would happen if we did send them to the cities? Would their futures still be decided? Don't you have strict hierarchies here? If someone is born a red, then there are many things not permitted to them. They are the lowest of your classes. Can a black who is a brilliant soldier ever become a commander? Can a bronze who might be a clever politician or diplomat ever become an ambassador? No. They're fixed in their places just as we are.'

The Queen stood up, her chair falling to the ground behind her.

'I can see that there is no common ground between us,' she said. 'When you are willing to discuss things properly instead of just hurling insults at our way of life, then we might be able to pursue these talks. Until then, they are ended.'

She stalked to the door leaving her chair on the ground. Pettic noticed his earring did not cool as she walked away. So the gem he was looking for was with Princess Eloraine.

The delegates from the groundlings stood and began to walk to the other door in the throne room. Then princess Eloraine rose, picked up the chair her mother had tipped over and called, 'Wait. I'm interested in what you were saying. Perhaps I can have some influence with my mother. Come back and talk.'

The three men turned slowly and walked back to the negotiation table. Once they were there, Eloraine spoke again.

'Sit down. Now, let's discuss our way of life first. You mentioned we live a life of comfort. Yes, we do, but it's also a life of boredom. Because of the strict hierarchy we can't do so many things. I would like to paint, but art is restricted to the blues. My brother loves hunting, but we're not allowed to hunt except on special occasions when we're hunting a fugitive.'

'We don't have a problem with boredom, Your Highness,' said Natas. 'but some of our young men and women are discontented because they're not allowed to do the job they would like to do. What you're doing is wrong, forcing people into jobs they don't like.'

The discussions went on for a long time and it was getting dusk when the three representatives returned to Smithtown. The Princess seemed to have been at least partially convinced by their arguments and she promised to speak to her mother about it.

The next morning, a red messenger arrived to tell Pettic, Natas and Harip to return to the city. This they did and were escorted to the throne room where the Queen, Eloraine and Tromb were already seated.

Queen Kelle began.

'Sit down, will you. My daughter has been speaking with me. It seems she thinks perhaps you were right and we should not be treating each other in the way we have. I don't agree, of course, but I have decided to continue negotiations.'

The day went a little better than the previous one. It seemed Eloraine had managed to persuade her mother that some compromises must be reached. She pointed out how reliant the cities were on the groundlings. If the groundlings continued with their embargo, then those in the cities would starve.

After a long day, they agreed in general terms that the aerials would stop sending babies down to die, but instead give them to a family. They also agreed to stop taking children from their families at twelve years old and putting them with strangers to learn a trade they may not wish to pursue. In return, the groundlings agreed to initially send the goods ordered up to the cities.

To more easily continue the following morning, the aerials reluctantly agreed the three groundlings could stay overnight in the cites.

That evening there was a knock at Pettic's door. He opened it to find Eloraine standing there. His earring began to heat.

'Your Highness,' he said, and bowed. 'Please come in.'

'You have very nice manners, Pettic,' said Eloraine.

'That's what comes from being brought up in a Royal Palace.'

'You were? Tell me about it.'

Pettic told her all about his upbringing in the palace on his home world. She was fascinated by how the royalty differed from the goldwings on Aeris. She asked about it.

'Well you see, Princess...'

'Oh, call me Eloraine. We don't need to be formal here.'

'All right. Eloraine, on my world I have often heard my king say that his job is to serve the people. He's not superior to them, but their servant. It's his job to try to improve their lives and not better his own. This seems to be the opposite of what you people think.'

Eloraine sat with her brows furrowed,

'It's certainly a different viewpoint,' she said. 'My mother wouldn't agree though. She only sees our position as one of privilege and power. She could never see we should, or even could, make the lives of others better. Perhaps if I talked to her and work on her, she just might be able to do something about the rigid structure of the aerials. Other than that, I have little hope.'

'Even that would be better than nothing,' said Pettic, hope growing in his breast that he could improve the lot of the groundlings, if not immediately, but when this princess came to the throne.

The pair talked well into the night. Just before she left in the small hours, Eloraine said, 'I would like you to stay here on Faoor when the others go back. I like talking to you.'

The next morning, the negotiations resumed, and eventually they signed a treaty. There was no help in it for the people of the cities and their rigid hierarchy, but the groundlings did earn some extra freedoms, not least that they would be treated as human beings. This was largely due to Eloraine's intervention. She had done more thinking when she left Pettic, and, thanks to their discussions she decided the groundlings were in fact human and not just very intelligent animals.

Pettic was pleased to be staying on Faoor, although he did go back with the others when they descended. He wanted to be there when they gave the news of their successes. Harip left for Brewerstown to tell his people what they had gained.

Birds flew from town to town with the news, and there was a full three days when no work was done at all to allow the people to celebrate.

Pettic and Cledo left to go up to Faoor after the three days. The people did not want him to leave, but he insisted. He needed to be on Faoor if he were to get the gem and return to his own world. He still had to find out which of Eloraine's jewellery contained the gem, decide how he was to get it and then leave.

Pettic settled into the rooms he had been allocated. He had little with him except the few clothes Natas's wife gave him. He washed himself in water in a basin on the washstand. It was not particularly hot, but Pettic did not mind. He settled down to read one of the books in the room when Eloraine knocked at the door.

She entered and sat in a chair opposite him. He was aware of the warmth in his ear. So she still wore the jewel. He looked at her and tried to remember which of her many pieces of jewellery she had been wearing each time he had seen her. The gem was obviously in a much loved piece of jewellery.

This would make it harder to get it from her, both from the practical point of view, and also from the ethical. He did not want to hurt her by stealing a piece of jewellery that she loved.

He was torn. He needed that gem in order to save his land. Would she give it to him if he asked her?

Elorane began speaking.

'Pettic, I've done a lot of thinking. I've had three days while you were gone and have decided you're right. The groundlings are obviously the same as us. They sometimes have winged babies, we sometimes have babies with no wings. I don't know what would happen if an aerial and a groundling were to mate. That would be interesting, wouldn't it?'

'I hope you aren't thinking of forcing some to try it!'

'Of course not. Don't be silly. I've learned it isn't good to force people to do what they don't want to do. No, I've come here to tell you of a decision I've made.'

Pettic stroked Cledo's ears as he listened. The dog leaned against his master's chair enjoying the experience.

Eloraine continued.

'I will be Queen after my mother. There's no way that I can get her to change things any more drastically than she already has. She does nothing but complain about how she was backed into a corner.'

Pettic stopped stroking Cledo who looked at his master in disappointment, nudged his hand twice, to no avail, then lay down on his feet.

'When I become Queen, though, I'll make some big changes. Eventually I want everyone to be free to work and live as they please. I'll allow the aerials to move up the hierarchy, regardless of wing colour. I'll allow the groundlings to come and work and live in the cities if they wish, and I'll allow the aerials to live and work on the ground, at whatever they choose.'

Pettic smiled. He almost jumped up and embraced the princess, but he remembered just in time that princesses are not fond of being grabbed in big hugs by their subjects.

Eloraine was continuing.

'It may be, that living and working together, aerials and groundlings may fall in love with each other. At present, marriage is not allowed, but I will allow it. Groundlings and aerials will be free to marry if they so wish.'

Pettic was sitting with his mouth hanging open. Eloraine had come much further than he could have imagined. From being a typical aerial she was now a radical. How would her subjects take it when she came to the throne?

'Pettic...I...I...well, one thing I would like,' she paused. 'Will you stay here on Faoor? Will you be a friend to me and help me? It will be hard for me to convince others. And...Oh, this is difficult. I would like us to be the first aerial and groundling couple.'

Pettic could not move. This was the last thing he expected. Princess Eloraine was probably the most beautiful woman he had ever seen, but he kept on seeing the face of another princess. A princess he had grown up with since he was thirteen. A princess who he was helping to find her brother. A princess who was naturally kind and understanding and who did not need anyone to tell her what was right and wrong.

'I'm flattered, Eloraine,' said Pettic, 'but I can't stay here forever. I'm here for a purpose and when that purpose is done, I must leave. I need to save my prince or my country will suffer greatly.'

Eloraine stood up. She spread her arms showing the beautiful golden membrane.

'Do you not find me attractive then?' she said.

'Eloraine, you are the most beautiful woman I have ever seen, or probably ever will. If I didn't have to go home to save my land, I'd stay here like a flash, but I have my duty.' *And Lucenra,* he thought. *I didn't realise it before, but she's very important to me.*

Eloraine sat down, head bowed.

'I shouldn't have said anything.' She spoke softly. 'Of course you must do your duty.' She raised her head then and looked him in the eyes. 'You can come back and visit, though. You can come through the arch in the garden. Perhaps when you've saved your prince you can come back to me.'

Pettic made no reply. He could not give her false hope, but then again he could not bring himself to tell her that he would not be back.

Eloraine pulled herself together and said, 'I'll write a contract and sign it. I'll get groundling and aerial witnesses, and you, of course, to sign too. Then I can't get out of doing what I've told you I intend.

'Please don't tell my mother about what I'm planning to do when I become queen. She might just decide to disinherit me.'

Two weeks later, Pettic, Natas and another groundling Pettic did not know went into Eloraine's private offices. There were three aerials there as well. A redwing, a bronzewing and a silverwing. All were young.

Eloraine entered and the signing began. Each of them read the documents spread out on the table and signed them, then the princess added her name.

'That's done then,' she said. 'Now I'm going to put these documents into a box, sealed with my seal.' She did as she said. 'Now this box will go into my safe and no one else knows the combination. My mother will never know of my pledge to all the people.' She matched her actions to her words and closed the safe.

'Now you are all dismissed. Pettic, you stay, please.'

Pettic wondered what was coming now. When everyone had left, Eloraine removed a diamond pin from her dress.

'I want you to have this, Pettic, to remind you of me when you return home. I suppose you'll want to go as soon as you can. I think you probably need to search the other cities for this gem you need. Oh, and here is your sword that we took from you before we sent you down to the ground.'

With that, she fled the room.

Pettic was amazed. Not only because the princess had given him her precious pin, but that as soon as he received it, his earring became extremely hot. Here was the gem he was looking for. A beautiful diamond. Of course, its clarity would represent air, just as the emerald represented the green of the plants on Terra and the ruby, the fires of Ignis.

Now he could at last go home.

The next morning Pettic and Cledo walked into the palace gardens. He wore the pin Eloraine had given him, but he wore it behind the lapel of his shirt just in case someone recognised it and thought he had stolen it.

He reached the arch and grabbed Cledo by the scruff of his neck. They passed through the arch into a mist and stepped out on the other side into a familiar place.

A sheep, grazing near the arch, jumped and ran away bleating at seeing Pettic and Cledo appear. Pettic laughed and then jumped as a figure approached. It was Princess Lucenra.

'Luce!' he exclaimed. 'What are you doing here?'

The princess smiled. 'I just came up on the off-chance you would be coming through.'

Lucenra patted Cledo who seemed pleased to see her, then she looked at Pettic and said, 'Father's lifted the banishment. The two girls, when they heard you'd been banished, told the Duke it was Torren who had instigated the game of strip poker and you tried to stop it. The Duke came and told father and he rescinded the banishment. That was six months ago. Since then we've been waiting for you to come back from your "business trip." '

'And what about Cledo? He did attack Torren. That much is true.'

'His sentence has been suspended. The girls said he was protecting them, and so he's one more chance, but if he attacks anyone again, then he will be destroyed.'

190

'Now I need this whole story,' said Lucenra as they walked back to the city.

'When we get back,' said Pettic. 'Have you been coming up to the standing stones often?'

The princess looked down at her feet. 'I've come up at some time every day,' she told him.

'How did you know what time to come up?'

'I didn't,' she said. 'I just guessed or came up when I could. Sometimes it was only for a half hour, but one day I managed six hours.'

'You stayed waiting for six hours?' he said, stopping to look at her and raising his eyebrows. 'From winter to summer? Is it the same year I left? You look no different.'

'Yes, it's been 6 months since you went. Pettic. How long were you on Aeris?'

'Probably about eight or nine months. Time wasn't so different this time, then?'

The pair soon arrived at the palace gates. The guard on duty saluted as they passed through. They went up to Pettic's apartment where Lucenra said she would send for some hot water so he could have a bath and be changed before meeting the princess to talk about his adventures in the world of Aeris.

He lay back in the bath luxuriating in the hot water until it started to feel cold, then he got out and had a shave.

He was just brushing his hair prior to performing the same task for the dog when he heard a knock at the door.

Lucenra, entered his apartment at his call. 'I hoped you were ready, Pettic, I couldn't wait to see you and the gem.'

Pettic held out the pin for her to see.

'Oh, that's beautiful,' exclaimed the princess. 'A diamond. A crystal clear diamond for the clear air. Now, tell me about your adventures on Aeris.

She sat down in a chair and motioned for Pettic to sit opposite her. He looked at her face and her eyes held his. An exquisitely beautiful face momentarily appeared in his imagination, but the familiar face of Lucenra soon eclipsed that of Eloraine. Lucenra was pretty while Eloraine was beautiful, but Pettic thought that Lucenra's inner beauty far outstripped the outer beauty of the aerial princess. He smiled.

'What are you smiling at?'

'I'm so glad to be here, and to see you, Lucenra.'

Lucenra blushed, but then said, 'I expect you'll be glad to see the others too. Now, tell me about your time away. What happened? Was the diamond difficult to get? What was Aeris like? Was it dangerous?'

'Woah,' laughed Pettic. 'One question at a time please. Aeris is a very interesting world.' He began to tell her of all that had happened.'

Chapter 18

That afternoon the king summoned Pettic. He entered the small throne room and bowed. His eyebrows rose as he saw a small gathering of courtiers there as well as the queen and all the royal children except for the Crown Prince. He bowed deeply to the king and queen, and less deeply to the royal children. The youngest one, a boy who had been born only three years previously, developed a fit of giggles as Pettic bowed to them.

'Why Pet bow?' he asked and was shushed by the queen.

Then the king got down from his throne and bowed to Pettic. The young man was confused. The king should not be bowing to him! Then the king spoke.

'My Lord, Earl of Flindon, I, King Horraic the second, offer my sincerest apologies to you for banishing you. It seems I was mistaken in what I had been led to believe and that you were innocent. Your dog, Cledo is likewise reprieved, but only on condition he does not make any further attacks. Any other attacks will result in his being put down.

'The true culprit in this case has been banished to a monastery for one month in order to contemplate the wrongs of his deeds. I will not have innocent young girls compromised while I am ruling this land.'

The king then returned to his throne and dismissed the assembled courtiers. As Pettic turned to leave along with them, the king called him back.

'I did that formally, Pettic, so the whole court can see you are innocent. I will not have anyone saying an innocent man is guilty of something he has not done. I'm ashamed of Torren, that he should have been so wanton.'

The king seemed to think for a moment and then said, 'Torren doesn't seem to have been himself for a while now. I think it's mixing with those guard friends of his. Some of the guards are a bit rough. When he comes back, Pettic, I'd like you to try to re-establish your friendship.'

The queen stepped down from the dais where she had been listening.

'We've noticed you and Torren seem to have become estranged,' she said. 'Whether that's due to an argument or just growing apart we don't know, but we prefer your influence to that of the guards. They're getting him into drinking, gambling and womanising and that's a worry for the future king.'

Pettic bowed to the King and Queen and told them he would do his best to do as they asked. He agreed Torren had not been himself, but did not know why. There had been no falling out between them except for the argument over the girls and playing strip poker.

Later that day, Lucenra came to see Pettic.

'We should take that pin to Blundo,' she told him. 'It needs to be with the sword. It's very valuable and anyone could steal it if they know it's here, then we'd be unable to rescue Torren from the Bubble.'

Pettic agreed, and the pair climbed the now familiar stairs to Blundo's quarters.

The magician rose as Princess Lucenra and Pettic, Earl of Flindon entered his tower laboratory.

'Your Royal Highness, Your Lordship.' He bowed to each of them in turn.

'Pettic has the gem from Aeris,' Lucenra told him.

Pettic held out the diamond pin still on his lapel. He unpinned it and Blundo took it.

'I'll put it with the sword then,' he said. 'Was it very hard to get?'

'Pettic had to foment a revolution on Aeris,' the princess told him. 'It was right that he did so, though. I think Aeris is a much better place now for everyone concerned.'

The three sat down and Blundo asked Pettic to tell him of his adventures.

When he finished, Blundo said, 'Well, I agree with the princess that you had to do that. You couldn't leave those poor groundlings as slaves.'

'They were worse than slaves,' Pettic told him. 'They were treated like animals. In fact the aerials believed they were animals, or at best, little better. I hope they've learned more now. I think Princess Eloraine was learning. She'll be the next queen of Faoor, so they should be better treated under her rule.'

Princess Lucenra scowled at the mention of Eloraine, but said nothing.

'You deserve a little rest before you go on your next adventure,' Blundo told him. The next full moon isn't until three weeks' time. You've just missed it this time round.'

The princess and earl descended the stairs and returned to her quarters. Once there, the princess sat down and ordered some wine for them both.

While they waited for the wine to arrive, Lucenra turned to Pettic.

'And is she very beautiful?' she asked him.

'Who? Oh, Eloraine. Yes, she's the most exquisite woman I've ever seen, or am likely to see.'

'And is it true the aerials wear no clothes?'

'Well, they would find it difficult with the membranes joining their arms and feet.'

Lucenra pouted. 'I suppose so,' she said. 'Still, you saw a lot of her in more ways than one.'

'You aren't jealous by any chance?'

'Jealous? Don't be stupid. Why would I be jealous?'

Pettic grinned a mischievous grin.

'Because she is more beautiful than you?' he said.

Lucenra's eyes narrowed as she picked up a cushion and threw it, with surprising accuracy, at Pettic. It hit him right in the mouth.

'That serves you right for grinning like that when I'm upset,' said Lucenra.

Pettic picked up the cushion and handed it back to the princess.

'She may be more physically beautiful than you, but there is more to beauty than what you see. You are a much more beautiful person than Eloraine ever could be.

The End of Book 1.

Will Pettic be able to find the gems on the other Elemental Worlds? Will he be able to rescue Prince Torren, and if he does, how will he manage to ascertain without doubt which young man is the true prince to the satisfaction of the rest of the court?

Read Book 2 to find out.

Reviews are very important to authors. If you have a few spare minutes, I would be very grateful for a review. It does not have to be long and complicated, just a simple reason why you either liked or did not like this book.

Thank you.

You can contact me on my website,
http://aspholessaria.wordpress.com/
Twitter @VM_Sang
Facebook www.facebook.com/Carthinal

I would like to thank all at Creativia for their help especially Miika Hannila who has been a great support in bringing this book to fruition.

About the Author

I was born and lived my early life in Cheshire in the north west of England. My father died while I was very young and my mother remarried. My stepfather was a farmer on the Cheshire/North Wales border. My step brothers and sisters all went to boarding school, but I was lucky enough to escape that, going to live with my mother's elder sister and her husband in order to get a good education. I passed my 11+ examination and went to Grammar School, thus getting a more academic education.

I have always loved books and reading. I learned to read before I went to school. The earliest book I remember was one about two little pandas whose Great Aunt Patsy gave umbrellas. They gave them away to aid a rabbit whose burrow was leaking and a bird whose babies were getting wet in the nest. It was in rhyme, and my mother told me I knew it off by heart and would say it along with whoever was reading it to me.

I loved Enid Blyton books. I know she's not supposed to be good, but she certainly got me reading. I loved her Famous 5 books and the Adventure books, like the Sea of Adventure, the Mountain of Adventure etc. There was another book by Enid Blyton, called Shadow the Sheepdog that I loved. This inspired me to write my very first story. I could not have been more than about 6 or 7, because I know I spelled 'of' wrongly throughout. I spelled it 'ov'.

I loved Black Beauty too, but was not impressed by Alice in Wonderland at all.

During my teenage years I wrote some poetry, one of which was published in the magazine of the University of Manchester Institute of Science and Technology (UMIST). Unfortunately, that is the only one that is still around.

I became a teacher and taught English and Science at my first school. My main subject was science, though, although I also taught Maths and what was then known as Computer Studies.

I was introduced to fantasy by a little 9 year old boy with the wonderful name of Fred Spittal who told me I should read The Lord of the Rings, but first read The Hobbit. This I did and have been hooked ever since.

I did little writing until I started teaching in Croydon, Greater London. Here I started a Dungeons and Dragons club in the school where I was teaching. I used bought scenarios at first, then thought I could write my own, which I did. The idea of turning it into a novel formed but I did little about it until I took early retirement. Then I began to write The Wolves of Vimar Series. Not having written a novel since my teens (a rather bad romantic novel) for the consumption of my friends, I was surprised at how this work seemed to take on a life of its own, and what was supposed to be a single novel turned into a series.

Walking has always been one of my favourite pastimes, having gone on walking holidays in my teens. I met my husband walking with the University Hiking Club, and we still enjoy walking on the South Downs. We also bought a kayak and have done quite a lot of kayaking in Brittany along the river Vilaine and the Oust.

Quieter things that I enjoy doing are a variety of crafts, such as card making, tatting, crochet, knitting etc. I also draw and paint.

I am married with two children, a girl and a boy. My daughter has three children and I love to spend time with my grandchildren. They are so much fun. I now live in East Sussex with my husband.

CPSIA information can be obtained
at www.ICGtesting.com
Printed in the USA
BVHW042321190121
598054BV00024B/505/J

9 781034 257806